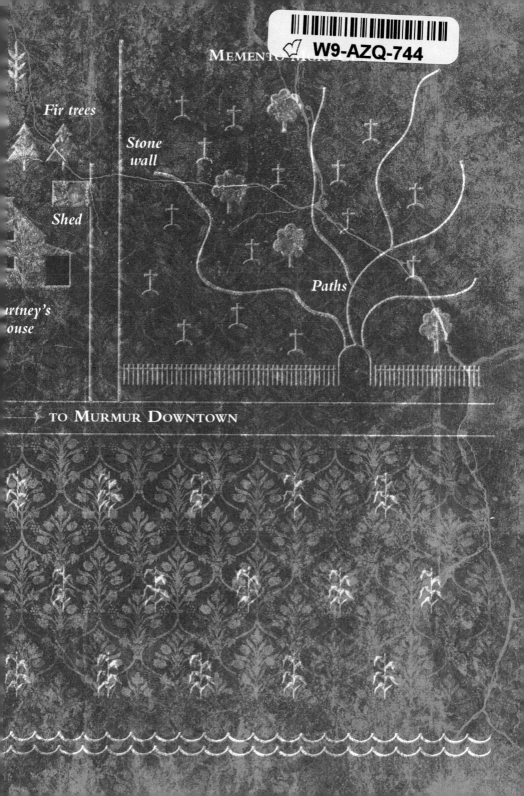

Love
To Taylor

Halloween 2008

Grandaddy Mike
+ G'ma Karen

CREEPERS

CREEPERS

Joanne Dahme

RP | TEENS
PHILADELPHIA · LONDON

Library of Congress Control Number: 2007942766

ISBN 978-0-7624-3313-1

Cover and interior illustrated and designed
by Frances J Soo Ping Chow
Edited by Kelli Chipponeri
Typography: Aperto, Bembo, Copperplate,
Porcelain, and Selfish

Running Press Book Publishers
2300 Chestnut Street
Philadelphia, PA 19103-4371

Visit us on the web!
www.runningpress.com

For
**VICTORIA
BROWNWORTH,**
my teacher and friend, who made the
miracle of this book happen.

And to
my writing mates,
DIANE, JANE, & LISA,
who provided
endless encouragement.

OPEN HOUSE SUNDAY 1:00-4:00 p.m.

This charming stone house, dating back to the eighteenth century, has been completely refurbished with new hardwood floors, and its stonework lovingly restored. At a price that may appear a steal, this home is waiting for the right family. Quiet location, surrounded by woods, cornfields, and an historic cemetery, it is a nature lover's and history buff's dream. This realtor, who is the current owner, cannot understand why it has yet to be a keeper.

chapter 1

THE FIRST THING I NOTICED WAS THE IVY, NOT THE sun-bleached tombstones with their off-white color, which jutted from the cemetery grounds like old bones. We moved into our house just a week ago, and when we pulled into the driveway behind the moving van, I saw that the ivy was everywhere—twisting up the trunks of the trees and dribbling across the lawn. Its vines clung to the old stone house and the leaves displayed various shades of green as they fluttered in the light August breeze.

"What's with all the ivy?" I asked my parents. They were staring at it, too.

My mother cleared her throat and gave a surprised little laugh. She looked at my dad to catch his expression, but he was already getting out of the car to direct the guys in the moving van.

"It's English ivy, Courtney. It's an exotic plant. It's the same ivy you see on the walls of castles and universities.

You know, like the ivy league colleges," she said with a little chirp in her voice, as if the connection had just occurred to her.

I opened my door and stood beside the car to get a better look at it. "Well, I don't like it hanging all over our house like that. It's sort of creepy."

She was leaning against the car now, too, watching my dad as he instructed the guys with the big muscles to be careful with the furniture.

"Well, it's known for its ability to spread quickly," she said, turning to smile at me. "Don't worry, I'll ask your dad to cut it away from the house after we're settled. Although. . . ."

She paused for a minute as she stared at the front door. A couple of vines seemed to be sunning themselves on its worn stone steps.

"*Hmmm*," was all she added.

Dad was right behind us and recognized the potential tripping hazard. He tackled the job as he does everything, without asking for direction or assistance. He talks to himself, though.

"Jeez, this stuff is incredible," I could hear him grumble as he yanked at a strand that was twisted around the front stair railing.

The branches made tiny popping sounds as he yanked

at the roots of the vines that trailed all the way to the corner of the house by the driveway.

"Ivy can damage the mortar between the stones," he announced to no one in particular. "We'll need to remove it." My mom shrugged and smiled at the movers.

It was a hot and sticky day, and I could see that Dad's T-shirt was stained with sweat. The ivy must have been holding on to the stones and mortar with all its might, the way Dad was tugging at it. His face screws up like a little kid's when he's frustrated.

He was working like a maniac, grabbing handfuls of vines and shoving them into a big plastic bag almost the same camouflage color of the ivy. I knew I should help him, but first I had wanted to check out the ivy in the cemetery.

I stepped over some vines, careful to avoid them like cracks in sidewalk pavements. *What did we like to say in the little kids' game I had played with friends? Step on a crack and you'll break your mother's back?* I wondered what we would have said about the ivy vines all over the yard. *Step on a vine and you'll kill time?*

I crossed my arms and rested my chin on the stone wall that separated our yard from the cemetery. The ivy vines were everywhere—creeping in all directions across the grass and the winding gravel paths to rest on the long-ago-collapsed mounds settled beneath the shadows of the tombstones. The ivy looked more natural in the cemetery.

"Courtney, could you grab another bag for me?" Dad yelled.

"Okay," I called back, slightly annoyed. Why did he have to tackle everything right away? I felt like the ivy and I were still getting acquainted.

By the following Saturday, Dad still had not made much progress with the ivy, which was considered an outside chore and therefore under Dad's responsibility area until he relegated gardening chores to me. Mom had him beat with the inside tasks. Within a week she had the furniture arranged, the curtains hung, the pots and the pans in cabinets or on hooks, and boxes placed in their respective rooms. There were a few boxes marked WINTER STUFF that were stored in the basement.

I was sitting on the stone wall that separated our yard from the cemetery, watching my dad toil while waiting for my mom. I had told her that I would go to the supermarket with her, since I had nothing better to do. It was sunny and hot, and the ivy was all over the cemetery again.

Little rivers of it flowed over the grassy mounds or twined around the old gravestones. Single vines of it dangled from the branches of trees like plastic bags snagged in the wind. I squinted at some leaves swaying from the nearest tree. They seemed to be trembling even though I couldn't feel even the smallest breeze.

Was the ivy there when we had first looked at the house last May? I could not remember, although I purposely had not paid a whole lot of attention to the cemetery. When my mom had told me that we would be living next to a crop of tombstones in addition to fields of corn, all I could think about were the millions of scary movies I had seen— withered hands thrusting through the dirt to lunge for ankles—but after a week I was getting used to the vines. Looking at the moonlit cemetery from my bedroom window gave me a different perspective. The cemetery was quiet, almost asleep. It looked magical with the tombstones reflecting the moonlight like stars. And in the gauzy glow, the ivy was invisible—either blending in with the dark green landscape or shriveling up at night like morning glories.

Unlike those movies, the cemetery I saw from my window at night was not stocked with zombies or ghosts, but instead remained respectfully calm, with only the sound of the cicadas filling the air. My mom liked to tell me how your mind can play tricks on you when you were staring at something that is supposed to be scary. The scene that I gazed upon over the past week had nothing to offer except for the hundreds of somber stones that seemed to meditate beneath the moonlight. Perhaps the ivy did indeed crawl up to sleep there, it was so quiet.

"Hey, Courtney! I could use a little help here." My dad's voice broke my concentration. He was attacking the ivy again, this time on the side of the house facing the cemetery. The ivy seemed to crawl up the side of the chimney. He held a pair of shears in his hand like a weapon as he squared off to confront it. I could not help but laugh at his face, streaked with sweat and dirt. He looked annoyed, though—always such a serious guy.

"I'll be with you in a few minutes, Dad. I'm just getting my bearings here."

He shrugged and shook his head, the same way he does when my mom puts him off. I know he did not have a clue about what I was talking about. I am not sure I did either. I just wanted to remember whether or not the ivy had been in the cemetery all along.

I was so focused on the ivy—its yellow veins glowing against the dark green underbelly of its leaves—that I did not see the older man and the girl enter the cemetery. An old black fence surrounded the cemetery, except for its stone border with our yard. Whorls of acorns and fruit were welded between its rails for decoration and there were a number of gates that led to various walking paths in the cemetery. I heard the clang of the iron gate and saw that the man and the girl had entered one only a few hundred yards down the road from our driveway. I squinted into the sun to get a better look at them. The man was holding what looked like a bundle of brochures.

I guessed the man was going to lead one of the cemetery tours that my mother had read about at the Murmur Information Center. She had been excited when she learned that this was one of the oldest cemeteries in the country and that tours were given to show the Puritan carvings on the tombstones. The guy looked at his watch and touched the girl on her shoulder. They began walking up the path that led toward the cluster of tombstones not far from our wall.

Normally I would stop staring. I am never outright rude and my mom would have been appalled, but I was almost hypnotized by the man and the girl—and the ivy. Suddenly they made a threesome. The ivy was no longer swaying. It seemed to be holding its breath at their approach. They were the only living things in the cemetery.

They stopped a mere hundred yards from me. The man noticed me as he stopped to kneel by a tombstone and gave me a friendly wave. He did not seem to think it odd at all that some girl would be sitting cross-legged on the cemetery wall.

This guy was probably much older than my own dad, who is in his mid-thirties. His hair was sort of gray and he wore those big black glasses that make your eyes look cartoonish. He wore a nerdy short-sleeved plaid shirt and jeans with black shoes.

Then she looked into my eyes. She just stared at me until I made my own sort of dorky wave. Then she turned away, like I was invisible.

The girl looked about my age, although in appearance she was my opposite. Her skin was very pale, as if she never went outside in the sunlight. She had very dark hair, almost black, and she wore it in two braids that dropped down her back, thick and heavy like rope. I could not see the color of her eyes, but I could see that they were large in contrast to her face. She was thin and almost fragile looking—like those porcelain figurines you see in china closets. Or maybe it was the slow and careful way that she moved that made her appear delicate. The man put his arm around her, tucked the brochures under his other arm, and gave her a playful squeeze. I realized they were probably grand-father and granddaughter by her tolerant expression and his expectant one. Maybe they were visiting the grave of her grandmother.

I turned away then, feeling like I was intruding on a private family moment. Even I got embarrassed at some point, staring like I was from my spot on the wall. *What is it about Murmur, Massachusetts that made me act and feel so strangely?*

———

When my mom told me that we were moving into this house, she took me for a ride to show it off. She said that if I saw it, she *knew* I would love it. The house is big, made of gray stone, and three stories tall, if you count the basement, which is partially above ground. It was built in 1719 and looks like many of the old houses in New England. Every room had large, lead-glass windows. The roof sloped nicely around the triangular, gabled windows, and there were two huge stone fireplaces—one in the living room and one in the dining room. The wood trim around the windows and doors had been freshly painted a forest green. The house was big but cozy—a great place to be stuck inside during a snowstorm. I pictured afternoons sipping hot chocolate and reading a good book next to one of the grand fireplaces.

The house had been unoccupied for a long time and it was part of an estate. When it was originally built, it served as the gatehouse for the cemetery, where the people who managed the cemetery lived. My mom shared that last little fact under her breath, like she was hoping to slip it by me.

I was excited when I saw that the house had an immense cornfield just across the road and woods on its north and west sides. I loved nature, to hike and to explore. I remembered thinking, *If only the house did not have that cemetery on one side of it.* If I happened to be awake at dawn, I could watch the sun rise behind a sea of floating tombstones, but I did not plan to get up early if I could help it.

I convinced myself that this would be a good move. I was beginning high school and many of the kids would be new to one another. I also liked the idea of a fresh start. My closest friends from home were either moving away or going to different high schools. We were all being separated and I did not like the idea of going to the neighborhood high school without them. I might have been convinced that everything was perfect until I noticed that sign on the cemetery's wrought-iron fence as we pulled out of our driveway and paralleled the cornfield, which spread over the horizon like an amber ocean.

Memento Mori had been welded like an arch over the cemetery's main entrance.

"What does that mean?" I had asked my mom.

"'Remember death'," she replied, glancing at the gate and the expanse of the cemetery beyond. "When this cemetery was active, that was all anyone could think about."

"Is that because people died young back then?" I asked.

"*Mmm-hmm.*" She nodded thoughtfully. "Life was so much harder. There were no medicines. People didn't eat as well. The climate was harsh." My mom's face was scrunched in concern. "It must have been difficult," she whispered, as if talking to herself.

"Let's change the subject," I suggested, staring into the hypnotizing rows of swaying cornstalks.

"'As I am, so thou shall be'." She seemed unable to stop herself from speaking. "I read that quote in the brochure at the information center. The Puritans believed that cemeteries were meant to be constant reminders to the living about their own fate."

"Thanks, Mom. I get the picture." I sighed, looking out the window. "How about all that corn?"

As we walked into the store I told her that just because we lived on the other side of the cemetery wall, I did not want to remember death every day.

She paused to grab a cart and looked at me as if I was kidding. "Of course," she agreed. "Do you have the list?"

My mom switched gears quickly. I watched her as she examined the cantaloupes piled in slanting stacks on the produce counter. Her straight blond hair had fallen across her eye, but she was oblivious. Instead, she brushed at her glasses as if they were the problem. Their light blue frames brought out the blue of her eyes. She was still tan from our week at the shore. Except for the laugh lines, her title for them, she could have passed for twenty. At thirty-five, that was pretty good. Some people thought that we looked so much alike, they asked if we were sisters. My mom loved it when that happened, although I think the senior citizens were just trying to be funny.

Already I was cold. Goose bumps were springing up all over my arms. I hate the way they blast the air-conditioning in grocery stores. You always feel as if you are in a freezer.

"Should I get the ice cream and milk?" I wanted to get out of there as fast as we could. I noticed then that my mom had a sweater tied around her waist.

She must have seen me eyeballing it. "Do you want to borrow this, Courtney?" she asked as she tugged at its sleeve. "It's chilly in here."

"No, I'm fine." I tried to sound annoyed. "I'm just

bored. I'll run down to the frozen food section. Can't be any colder than this."

She just shook her head as I maneuvered down the row, dodging families with overflowing carts and an old couple with a small basket. The aisles were clogged with mothers and their children or older people for whom food shopping was like a pleasant Sunday drive. The frozen food section was six aisles over and fortunately it was not too crowded.

I was just about to reach for a gallon of rocky road, when a man's voice called from behind me, "Oh, miss." I turned around and there was that old man with the glasses that looked like magnifying lenses, holding a few cans of cat food in one hand and the twenty items or less basket in his other.

"Excuse me?" I ventured. I checked to see if some other "miss" might be standing near me.

He nodded and gave me a surprisingly nice smile, showing all of his teeth, which looked to be in good shape. He seemed suddenly younger when he smiled, despite his gray hair. Maybe he was not the girl's grandfather after all.

"Aren't you the young lady who moved into that wonderful old house next to the cemetery?" he asked pleasantly. He put his basket on the floor as if he expected a long conversation.

"Uh, yes," I replied. I hated it when I stammered, but I was unsure how honest I should be. Just because I had seen him in the cemetery did not make him less of a stranger.

He extended his hand to shake mine. It was hard, callused, and strong. "My name is Christian Geyer. I give tours of the cemetery as a volunteer." He paused, waiting for my name.

"I'm Courtney . . . O'Brien," I stammered, mesmerized by his enormous eyes floating behind those lenses. I looked at him closely and could see that he did not have many wrinkles. He was probably in his fifties. Lots of my friends at home had dads who had celebrated their fiftieth birthday. He did not look much different from them. He needed to color his gray hair and ditch the glasses, though, to really pass for a friend's dad.

"I saw you and your daughter . . . " He nodded at the question as I continued, ". . . in the cemetery earlier." *How did he get here so quickly?* I wondered.

"Oh yes, Margaret," he agreed, as if just remembering her. "You must meet Margaret. She will be so happy to have a new friend in the neighborhood. Margaret!" he yelled, before I had a chance to make an excuse to get back to my mom.

Margaret popped her head out from the end of the aisle, by the dog toys and leashes, as if she had been waiting for this entrance.

She was wearing the same khaki shorts and flowered T-shirt that she wore in the cemetery. She walked down the aisle real slowly, as if she could not expend the energy.

"Margaret, I want you to meet Courtney. She lives in the house next to the cemetery. We have a new neighbor," he said, looking at her again in that same anxious way that begged for a smile.

"Neighbor?" I asked. Either they lived in the corn-fields, the woods, or the cemetery. None of those choices looked very inviting.

Now Margaret did smile, a slow, smart one. "He means that in a general way," she explained. "Although we do spend lots of time at the cemetery."

Up close, she looked really beautiful. There was no color in her cheeks, but her green eyes against her pale complexion and midnight hair were amazing. The colors reminded me of the cemetery at night. I stared at her as I tried to imagine her life with Mr. Geyer. She did not seem embarrassed by him or annoyed that he made her do those cemetery tours. *What made her so different from the girls I knew?*

"Courtney?" my mom was now calling, from the sound of it, near the frozen food aisle.

"Over here, Mom." I wondered if my voice sounded as relieved as I felt.

She had her sweater on now and was pushing that cart like a jogging stroller. Her eyebrows arched in surprise when she saw me stranded with Mr. Geyer and Margaret.

I made some quick introductions and my mom appeared relieved. I think she smelled a story.

"You provide tours of the cemetery? I'd love to join you sometime and learn about its history. Perhaps I could do a feature on you?" she asked hopefully. She was always perkily pushy.

Mr. Geyer positively beamed. "That would be wonderful. Margaret and I are due to give a tour tomorrow at four o'clock as a matter of fact. Would that work for you?"

My mom's eyes widened in surprise. She probably did not expect Mr. Geyer to take her up on her offer so quickly. Margaret still wore a little smile, as if she were amused by her reaction.

"Tomorrow?" she repeated, mentally tallying the day's schedule. "Actually, that should work. Courtney and I would love to join you." She looked at me. "Right?" I did not say a word. "Where should we meet you?" she asked.

"Right by the main entrance. You won't miss us," he said as he turned to Margaret, who had slowly picked up the basket.

"Nice meeting you, Courtney." This time her smile seemed genuine. "Come on, Dad." She tugged at his arm.

"We don't want to be late for this afternoon's tour."

Mr. Geyer did a little bow. "Wonderful meeting you, ladies. Until tomorrow."

We watched as they walked down the aisle toward the cashiers. *Was that all they were buying? Ten or so cans of cat food?*

"Thanks, Mom," I mumbled sarcastically.

"Oh, Courtney. This could be fun. We should learn everything we can about our house and the neighborhood." She turned to look at the retreating pair one more time. "He must not be married, the way he dresses," she noted.

I just rolled my eyes.

"And this is great—you meeting a potential friend already, after barely a week."

Maybe, I thought, ignoring that little twinge in my stomach. I kept seeing Margaret's amused smile.

"Let's get the milk," I answered, pulling the cart forward.

The beautiful grounds
of the new cemetery are soon to
be peopled with the bodies
of our dead.
The time of the year when it is
practical to remove bodies from
the old burial grounds has arrived and
many removals will soon begin.
Town folk who have loved ones
in the old grounds
should begin the procurement of lots
in the new cemetery.

MR. MILLER, THE UNDERTAKER, WILL ATTEND
TO THEIR DECOROUS AND PRUDENT REINTERMENT.

chapter 2

I T WAS FOUR O'CLOCK AND I WAITED TILL THE VERY LAST minute to meet up with Mr. Geyer and Margaret. Mom was unable to make the tour after all. She had forgotten about a promise to meet her new friend Angela at the bookstore this afternoon and asked me to apologize to Mr. Geyer and reschedule if possible. She met Angela last week at the Murmur Library book lecture in town. Angela was a writer, too, and worked for the town's newspaper, *The Murmur Mercury*. Angela was going to help get my mom a freelancing job with the paper. I protested about going to the cemetery alone, but Mom was right. We did not know how else to contact him and my mom would never stand anyone up.

There was a wind blowing from the north as I walked along the grass swale on the side of the road. I could smell the sharp tang of rain and could hear the cornstalks on the other side of the road whispering as they brushed against one another. The clouds lay fat, low, and dark on the horizon. I almost felt relieved. Surely Mr. Geyer would cancel the tour with a thunderstorm looming over our heads. Otherwise, I was afraid that he would have talked me into joining them without my mom.

The iron gate was heavy and cried as I pulled it open. My plans were to meet them at the main entrance from *inside* the cemetery. I did not want to walk beneath that *Memento Mori* welcome sign if could help it.

I was only about five hundred yards from the main entrance when I saw Mr. Geyer and Margaret with their backs to the wind leaning against the gate's large iron post. I jogged between the gravestones, all of which were waist high. Some were square, some had semicircular tops, and some were capped with triangular shapes like a mountaintop. I did not have a chance to read the inscriptions. I considered them as more obstacles to get around rather than "points of interest," as a travel brochure might say. My sneakers hit the ground in a steady cadence and I made sure that I was not landing on top of anyone's grave.

It was while jogging that I heard the rustling. It reminded me of the sound of dead leaves when they are tossed and dragged callously along the ground by the wind. At first my feet were landing on short grass, browned by the past dry month. Then I noticed the strands of ivy that had weaved themselves along my path. From the corner of my eye, I could see the ivy crawling across the lawn and lolling over gravestones. It was everywhere, trying to act as a tripwire for my feet.

"Courtney! Are you all right?" Mr. Geyer reached for my shoulders to steady me, as if I might topple onto his shoes.

I was out of breath, running as if I had been chased. I looked down at my feet and then behind me to see if the ivy had retreated. Of course, its wiry shoots still filled the cemetery lawn like tiny veins.

"Yes, I'm fine," I squeaked nervously. I did my best to sound normal. "Mom couldn't make it. She wanted me to ask if she could arrange another date."

I could see Margaret eyeing me with interest. The wind blew the little wisps of her hair that were not long enough to be braided. She was wearing a pink shirt with white polka dots—a shirt I would not be caught dead in—but she looked beautiful.

"It's just as well. We would have to cancel with this weather anyway," Mr. Geyer replied pleasantly. Despite his coke-bottle lenses, he was squinting up at the sky, looking for a sign.

"Daddy, while we are here, can we show Courtney Prudence's grave?" Margaret asked sweetly. It was the first time she even looked like she was pleading. Her green eyes were wide and hopeful.

The wind was gusting now and the big trees in the cemetery were shaking their branches like castanets. Even the ivy appeared intimidated as it clung to the stones and shoots of the grass.

Mr. Geyer took a last look over his shoulder at the weather before he answered. "Yes, Margaret, but we had better hurry or we will be soaked."

Margaret surprised me by taking my hand. It felt smooth and cool.

"I'll show you," she whispered.

No one spoke as we followed a thin gravel path toward the center of the cemetery. The wind blew furiously, whipping the end of my ponytail across my cheeks. I looked toward my house and thought how tiny it appeared, cowering beneath the glower of the bilious black cloud hanging over the chimney. Its sides looked damp already, but I realized that it was the ivy that darkened its walls. Despite my dad's valiant efforts, it kept growing back.

"Here it is," declared Margaret, yanking my hand as we stopped in front of a thin gray tombstone that was tilted backward. The tombstone looked tired, as if we had caught it in the act of reclining.

I couldn't help but gasp as I looked at its face. On the

top of the stone in the dome was an hourglass with a bone leaning against each side. Beneath the hourglass was a smiling skeleton, with a laurel wreath around his skull. In one hand he held a beaming sun with squiggly rays of light. The other hand held what looked like an apple. The skeleton was in a circle made up of a snake that was swallowing its own tail. Two bats fluttered at the bottom of the snake circle, like bugs trying to reach the light. At the top were two angels with angry smiles. The bottom half of the stone surrounding the inscription was carved with swirling ivy.

"Here lies the body of

PRUDENCE GEYER,

beloved daughter of Christian,
who died in the
thirteenth year of her life.
1712."

Margaret read the inscription aloud. Her voice was soft and sad.

I looked at them both, trying to see what sort of reaction they were expecting, but neither of them was looking at me. They were staring at the tombstone.

"Was Prudence a relative of yours?" I asked. I knew it sounded stupid. "I mean, she has your last name."

"Prudence is an ancestor of ours, Courtney, although we are not direct descendants. She lived here perhaps eleven generations before us." He said it wistfully, like he was sorry he had not had the chance to get to know her. The wind was blowing his gray hair so that it seemed to be standing on top of his head.

"Tell her about Prudence, Dad. I want Courtney to know." Margaret slipped her hand into Mr. Geyer's. Her green eyes were serious as her gaze locked onto his face. Neither of them seemed to pay any attention to the far-away rumbling of thunder.

"What about Prudence?" I asked, a little too nervously. The ever-darkening clouds were making a fast approach.

Mr. Geyer took off his glasses and wiped the lenses against his shirt. His brown eyes, unmasked for the first time, looked sad and young. "You don't mind, do you Courtney? I'll be quick." He glanced at the sky. "Margaret doesn't let me share this story with most people." It was then that Margaret looked away from both of us.

For some reason, I felt suddenly important because Margaret deemed me worthy of such a secret.

"Of course I'd love to hear about Prudence," I said curiously.

"She lived in your house, Courtney. Well, in the house that shared the same foundations as yours," he amended when he saw the look of surprise on my face. "The original caretaker's house burned in 1712. Prudence's father, who was also named Christian, was a stonecutter and carved many of the tombstones in this cemetery. He lived in that house until his death."

I could feel Margaret studying my face as I quickly scanned a few gravestones. "Do you mean he cut the stones?" I asked.

Mr. Geyer nodded. "Yes, that's right. He cut the stones and also carved the inscriptions and the symbols that you see on their faces. Death was extremely important, as it still is in our lives." He sort of laughed. "What I mean is, the stonecutters, like the first Christian, took it as their most important job to tell the life story of a person on the tombstone, giving comfort to the people left behind."

"Did he carve his daughter's stone?" I asked. I tried to imagine my father drawing a skeleton head as a sign of his love. Margaret must have seen the look on my face.

The growl of thunder was longer and lower this time. Only black clouds now hung over the cornfields' horizon but Margaret and Mr. Geyer were undeterred.

"Explain the symbols," Margaret instructed. "They *are* morbid unless you understand their meaning." I looked at

Margaret, a girl who used such grown-up words. She stood beside her father, oblivious of the wind that seemed to be shaking the trees to their foundations.

"A quick summary of the symbols for you, Courtney, before we, too, are blown away." He was louder now. The wind refused to be ignored.

He pointed at Prudence's tombstone. "The hourglass symbolizes the flight of time and the crossbones are for mortality. The skeleton is simply the head of Death, and you'll notice that he is crowned with a laurel, denoting his victory." Margaret squatted beside the tombstone now, peering at it as if it were the first time that she was examining it.

Mr. Geyer continued, "He holds in his hands the sun and the moon, which, according to the Bible, represent the new heaven and the new earth." He scowled for a moment while catching his breath. "Beneath him are two bats, which symbolize the evil of the world that death has conquered. And thank goodness for the smiling cherubs, which are meant to soften the otherwise gruesome effect of the engravings. The mourner is supposed to remember, above all else, that Death as the champion transforms us into happier and innocent beings once again."

"And the ivy?" I asked, truly interested now. "Is the ivy on the stone because it is everywhere? Sort of like a reminder of home?"

Mr. Geyer shook his head. "No, the ivy is different. . . ."

"Let me tell Courtney," Margaret interrupted. There was a weird urgency to her voice. Her eyes were bright although her face was pale and calm.

"Christian was heartbroken by his daughter's death, and even though he dealt with death every day of his life, he wasn't ready for it to take Prudence away from him. Isn't that right, Dad?" Margaret asked, more to add emphasis than for his confirmation, it seemed.

"Yes," Mr. Geyer agreed. His glasses were back on his face. His eyes, truly like saucers again, suddenly looked concerned.

"When Christian was carving Prudence's stone, he was approached by a woman from the town. She was rumored to be a witch, but Christian didn't care." Margaret's voice had dropped to a whisper. I no longer cared about the coming storm.

"She told Christian to carve ivy around the stone's border. It represented life, of course, as ivy is an evergreen, a plant that survives all seasons. The ivy was to bring Prudence back."

I was afraid to ask the question, but I did anyway. "Of course it didn't work, right?"

Margaret suddenly smiled sadly. "No, it didn't work. But soon the ivy was all over the cemetery. At least, that's what Christian's journals claimed. My dad read them all as a part of his research."

A crack of lightning made us jump. A moment later I felt the cold rain hitting my shoulders like pebbles.

"Let's go, girls. The tour is over for today," Mr. Geyer yelled, sounding relieved.

We were trotting now, down a gravel path toward the main entrance. I noticed that the ivy was everywhere.

"Is that why it's still here? The ivy, I mean?" I asked.

"We don't know," Margaret said simply. She was glistening now under a sheen of water. "That is part of the *mystery* we're looking to solve."

Lightning was cracking across the sky and Mr. Geyer said that it wasn't a good idea for us to be standing outside. They left me at the end of my driveway without explaining the mystery.

I was soaked and cold. My T-shirt was glued to my body and my jeans felt as if they weighed a ton. I watched Mr. Geyer grab Margaret's elbow as he shuffled her down the road, away from the cemetery. They looked so vulnerable, jogging gingerly along the grassy swale, which already had a little river of water racing along its path. The cornstalks on the other side of the road were leaning menacingly toward them, pressed by the wind. I thought of the cranky trees in *The Wizard of Oz* pitching their apples at Dorothy and her buddies.

"Do you want a ride?" I screamed after them. "I can ask my dad!" The thunder and wind working together were deafening.

Mr. Geyer waved off my offer. He pointed toward something farther down the road. If he had a car, why wouldn't he have parked it by the cemetery gate?

Another explosion of lightning jolted my body and I sprinted for our front door. The massive oak trees along our driveway seemed angry as they quaked in the wind, desperately shaking off the deluge like a wet dog. As I lunged for the door, it suddenly swung open. My dad stood in the foyer with a towel in his hand.

"Courtney, you're soaked!" He laughed despite himself. He had trouble being a tough guy with me. "Do you always have to wait until the last minute?" he asked, dropping the towel on my head and rubbing vigorously.

"Whoa, Dad. I can do it!" I didn't mean to sound annoyed as I pushed his hands away. It was just that I was still preoccupied by the story of Prudence, the witch, and the ivy.

"Okay, okay, sorry!" he shot back, raising his hands in the air. Even though he was thirty-six years old, he can suddenly look like a kid to me, with his red hair and freckle-covered face. He looked just like the kid in all the photographs taken of him when he was my age. This thought made me smile.

"It's okay," I said, chucking the towel at him. "I thought you were going to yank my head off."

He caught the towel and cocked his head. "You're still wet, Courtney. Go upstairs and change right now. Your mom will blame *me* if you catch a cold."

"I will. I just need to ask you a question first. Did you know that this house was built on the foundations of a house that burned down a long time ago?" I crossed my arms because I was shivering now, but I did not want Dad to know it.

"Where did you hear that?" he asked. He went to sit on the finished wood stairway, choosing the fourth step up so he could stretch his legs out. Since I crossed my arms, he must have thought that I was mad about something. "Your mom knows the most about the history of this house, but I don't remember the realtor mentioning it. It doesn't bother you, does it?"

"No, not really. I don't think so." I was unsure if it bothered me. I sat beside him on the stair. The stairway was wide enough for four people to sit across. "Mr. Geyer and Margaret told me. We live in the house of a girl who is buried in the cemetery. Prudence is one of their ancestors. Well, we live on the first house's foundations anyway."

"Really?" My dad looked at me in surprise, like he was interested, too. "We'll have to ask your mom when she gets home. I was so tied up with the office move that your mom took charge of a lot of the research for our new house."

He leaned toward me and placed his hand on my knee. "Are you sure you're not worried about something, Courtney? You seem a little shook up." He smiled sympathetically. "On a dark and stormy night, ghost stories can really creep a person out."

"I'm okay, Dad." I smiled back to prove it. "It's just that the house seems a little different now. I'll ask Mom when she gets home."

He nodded. "A house this old is bound to have some interesting history, and we're a part of it now."

"What part are the foundations? Is that the basement?" I could not get Prudence out of my mind.

My dad stood up, pulling me up by the hand. "Yep. I wouldn't be surprised if the entire basement was the original. The slate floor and the stone walls would probably have survived a fire." He handed the towel back to me. "Now go on up and put some dry clothes on while I pull something out of the refrigerator for dinner. Mom said she wouldn't make it home in time to join us."

"Okay." I wrapped the towel into a ball. I could not wait to change. I wanted to go into the basement—a room that Prudence once knew.

I could hear something sizzling on the stove as I crept down the basement steps. It was funny how I recognized that smell. Our basement back in Philadelphia, which was not half as old as this one, always felt cool and smelled of damp earth with a tinge of laundry detergent. My mom loved the smell. She said the musty aroma reminded her of museums and archives. She was weird that way.

I let my hand run along the smooth, cool stone of the wall. It was covered by a fine layer of dust but otherwise seemed clean. There were no spiderwebs or bugs. The single bulbs that hung from the ceiling seemed to glow against the dark instead of shine, but I could see fairly well. Not much was down here. A bunch of boxes were stacked in the far corner, and a faded sofa and a rocking chair were pushed against the front wall. Dad had insisted that it would be okay to store our winter stuff and knickknacks down here for a couple of weeks, even though Mom was worried about mold. Our washer, dryer, and utility sink were lined along the wall opposite me. The shadow of the heater and water tank seemed to lurk not far from the boxes.

I walked to the center of the basement, which was about ninety feet long and thirty feet wide. It obviously didn't extend under the entire house. Maybe the basement outlined the dimensions of what had been Prudence's house.

"Prudence." I did not mean to say it out loud. I'm not superstitious, but I could not stop myself from whipping my head around to check out all the corners. Nothing was there, but I touched my chin with my fingers to give the impression that I was calm and thinking, just in case anybody was watching.

I tried to picture the basement as Prudence would have seen it. The walls and floor would look the same, but what did her family keep down here? Jars of preserves like I've seen in movies? Maybe they kept their tools down here and equipment for the horses. Then I remembered what Prudence's father did for a living—a stonecutter, a grave marker, a caretaker for the cemetery. He was like a sculptor, and the basement could have been his workshop. Did he keep his stones down here until they were ready to be planted in the cemetery? Would any of his tools still be here?

Prudence was my age when she died. I began to slowly pace the floor of the basement. I was not going near any corners, but I was looking along the edges of the floor for pieces of broken stone. What were the tombstones made of? Margaret knew. She had mentioned slate, marble, and limestone. I paused and looked down at the smooth gray slate beneath my feet.

I thought about how Margaret had grabbed my hand to drag me to Prudence's grave. Why did Margaret care so much about Prudence? Was it because they were related? What about the almost three hundred years that separated them in time? How would I feel if I found out information about a girl or boy my age who was a part of my family centuries before I was born? I tried to imagine this and would have yearned to know more, especially if I would have seen a portrait of them or maybe something they wrote. Margaret had seen Prudence's tombstone—the skull, the snake, the bats, and the angels—perhaps she wanted to learn more about Prudence, or maybe it was the story about the ivy. Did she believe that the ivy could bring Prudence back to life? I shivered, as if I were soaked all over again.

I had reached our boxes without discovering anything

interesting. Those moving guys had really packed them in tight and piled them three rows high. I squinted to see what my mom had markered across their sides. A few of them screamed *FRAGILE!* because they contained plates, vases, or picture frames. Putting these items away was my mom's next project, she complained, after she found herself a writing job. She had looked at me sternly, as if to imply that I would be recruited to help. A box in the top row was mine. I saw my name scratched in red. I remembered I had packed my favorite flannel sweatshirt in just that box. My goose bumps reminded me that I could use it now.

I stood on the first row of boxes as I pulled mine from the wall and dropped it on the floor. Nothing fragile in this one, I told myself, as it landed with a thud. I was about to jump down and rummage through it when I noticed that a section of the wall, where the box had been, had some sort of markings on it. I leaned forward on the boxes to get a better look. At first I wished I had brought a flashlight, but by the way that my heart was suddenly thumping, I knew that my fingers were tracing what my eyes weren't seeing.

Ivy. Someone had carved delicate vines of ivy on the wall, whose tendrils curled like baby's hair. Some of the leaves were as long as my thumb, while others were budding shoots. Whoever had carved them here obviously took their time. The vines were etched deeply into the wall, while the veins of the leaves were fragile and precise. The vines appeared to snake down behind the boxes. Did Christian, Prudence's father, practice his art in the basement? The slap of thunder against the house caused the lights to flicker. I leaped from the boxes to sprint up the basement stairs.

"Dad!" I yelled as I slapped my palms against the basement door and burst into the kitchen. For a moment all I could do was stand there out of breath. The kitchen was huge. Slippery black-and-white tiles had been laid on the floor. My parents' prized copper pots and pans hung from the rafters. They liked to pretend that they were gourmet chefs. My dad was peering into the refrigerator. When my legs could move again, I practically sprinted across the floor to meet him.

"Courtney, be careful! What were you doing in the basement?" He was squatting with a head of lettuce in his hand.

"I just wanted to see if it had changed at all from the time Prudence was here," I panted. My heart was still threatening to beat right out of my chest. Should I ask my dad what he knew about witches and curses?

He tossed the lettuce into a bowl on the kitchen table and pulled out a chair. "The basement didn't change much,

I'm sure. It's obvious no one has ever renovated it, except to install plumbing and electricity for the house and the basement appliances." He began pulling the lettuce apart with gusto and motioned for me to take a seat. "Maybe we can make the basement one of my future projects. We can renovate it to create a game room or something. What do you think? Just because this house is old, it doesn't mean that we can't make any changes, as long as your mom agrees." He laughed.

I gave him a quick, insincere smile. I couldn't imagine Christian or Prudence liking the idea of an entertainment center and a Ping-Pong table sharing their space. Suddenly I did feel that it was truly theirs.

"What do you know about witches, Dad?" I blurted out.

He frowned for a moment. "Witches? *Hmmm*, I *knew* you shouldn't have gone to the cemetery in this bad weather."

"You're thinking of ghosts, Dad," I replied impatiently, although that notion had also crossed my mind.

"Oh," he said. "Well . . ." He brightened as he started tossing carrots and celery slices into the bowl. I could tell that he had decided to make light of the subject. He was so easy to read. "I know they dress in black and have long pointed noses with a wart on the end. And they travel by broom. How's that?" he asked proudly.

"Never mind," I said disdainfully. "I'll ask Mom when she gets home, or Mr. Geyer if I see him tomorrow." I grabbed one of the unchopped carrots and began to munch on it. Maybe it was just a weird coincidence, I told myself. Dad was not the right person to ask anyway. He did not take this kind of stuff seriously.

"That ivy is amazing," Dad announced. I looked up at him in surprise to see him staring out the kitchen's bay window. Ivy was drooping all over the glass, as if the rain were attempting to wash it away by making the window-panes too slick to grasp. As I stared at it, I almost thought that its leaves were cocking their faces at us in an appeal. *Let us in*, I imagined them begging.

"I pulled the ivy down on this side of the house just last week." Dad gave a little whistle. "You would never know it by the crowd at our window."

That was all I had to hear. I jumped up and snatched at the curtain cord, swishing them closed.

"Courtney, what is the matter with you? You're awfully jumpy tonight. I bet you're hungry," he said as he stood up and pushed out his chair, giving me a long, worried look before he walked to the oven.

"I'm fine, Dad. Like you said, just hungry." I tried to stare through the curtains, which were not quite sheer. The faintest of shadows could be seen behind them, shadows that were trembling against the rain. I vowed then that I would talk to Mr. Geyer and Margaret tomorrow about the ivy carvings covering the basement walls. Could the carvings be a clue to the mystery of Prudence—a mystery I still knew nothing about?

The MURMUR MERCURY

OCTOBER 31, 1958

Remembering Death on All Hallow's Eve

Mr. Elliot Travis, the owner of the eighteenth century cemetery gate house on Hickory Creek Road, conducted a chilling candlelight cemetery tour in honor of the Halloween season. Mr. Travis, dressed as a Puritan stonecutter, talked about the terrible 1712 fire that burned the original house to its very foundations. He shared, in a dramatic tone fit for the ghostly celebration, that town records noted that "the smoke from the fire was black as night and could be seen marring the sky from miles away." By the time that fellow towns people arrived, the roof and floorings of the house were gone and the stone walls were scorched and covered with thick layers of ash.

chapter 3

I DID NOT GET A CHANCE TO TALK TO MOM LAST NIGHT. She stayed out later than she had expected. She apologized as she gave me a quick kiss the next morning. I was still in bed, squinting at my closed curtains, searching for a hint of sun. Apparently, Angela, my mom's new friend, nabbed a part-time job for my mom at the newspaper, and she had to be out the door by seven o'clock. I would have to track down Mr. Geyer and Margaret to ask them about the ivy in the basement, I realized, still dazed from my mother's morning burst of energy.

I threw on some khaki shorts and a T-shirt and stumbled down the stairs. Not being a morning person, I grunted something at Dad when I saw him sitting comfortably at the kitchen table, finishing his cup of coffee before he went to work.

"Morning, Courtney. I guess you heard the good news about Mom?" he asked as he folded his newspaper. His hand automatically shot to the briefcase leaning against his chair.

"Uh-huh," I replied, closing my eyes against a blinding ray of sun. "Dad, do we have a phone book?"

He stood up to carry his coffee mug to the sink. "Phone book? Who are you going to call?" He looked at me quizzically, his eyebrows suddenly perched low over his sockets.

"I'm looking for Margaret Geyer's number. I was hoping I didn't have to hang by myself today." I knew that would get him.

His features softened. "As a matter of fact, I think we have a book right in this drawer." He pulled it open and proudly displayed his find.

"Thanks, Dad. You can leave it on the counter." I did not want to seem too anxious.

He grabbed his tie so it would not flop in my face when he bent to kiss me. "Okay, Court. You be good. You have my work number. It's on the refrigerator door."

"Yup. I know where it is."

"Don't forget you promised to do some weeding for me this morning. Just the flower beds in front and on the cemetery side." His hand was on the kitchen doorknob as he turned to smile.

Cemetery side, I thought. *We need to come up with a better name for that side of the house. Maybe something like "the wall of the east wing of the house."*

"I won't," I promised.

As soon as the door closed, I was standing at the counter, flipping through the G's, but I could not find the Geyers. *This town isn't that big.* I'd have to watch for them, and the weeding would give me a good excuse to hang outside.

After my bagel and milk, I went out front to check the weather and to retrieve Mom's gardening gloves. She always leaves them jammed by the roots of the last plant she worked on. That was why she always bought the brightest colors. I spied something red by the azalea bush along the front of the house on the east corner. Unfortunately the color didn't keep them dry. I was holding the gloves as far away from myself as I could, as they were extremely muddy and gross.

Annoyed, I stared up at the clear sky. The sun already looked like a radiating ball of heat. The bark of the trees was still dark from the rain, but I knew they would be dry in a matter of hours. If I was going to fulfill my promise, I had better garden now.

"Just going to pull up some weeds," I announced. I did not want the ivy thinking that I was coming after it.

After two sweltering hours of crawling around in those flower beds, without gloves, I heard the voice of Mr. Geyer. I turned to see them both walking by my driveway.

"Hey! Wait. Mr. Geyer! Margaret!" I jumped up without thinking, wiping my dirty hands on my shorts. They stood politely as I trotted down our driveway to meet them.

"Hi, Courtney," said Margaret as she smiled at me. Her hair was still in those braids that looked as if they had the sinewy strength of two shiny snakes. She was wearing a pink sleeveless shirt, white shorts, and brown sandals. Mr. Geyer was even wearing shorts—plaid, of course—and a blue polo short. He was wearing sandals, too, but with black socks. *Why did she let him out of the house that way?*

"Courtney, you look much drier than the last time we saw you." He laughed. His eyes thinned to long lines when he smiled, trapped behind those lenses. He held some brochures in his hand.

"Another tour scheduled?" I asked.

"There's always the possibility of a tour," Margaret answered for him. "Are you available for one today?"

"Um . . ." I did not want a full tour, just some quick answers to my question. "Maybe," I replied. "I have some weeding to finish first."

"What is it, Courtney?" Mr. Geyer interrupted with a gentle smile. "You have the look of a person bursting to ask a question."

"I do?" He seemed kind of nerdy, but this guy did not miss a trick. "Well, actually," I admitted, "I want to show you something." I turned to look back at the house. The ivy growing on its walls whispered in the breeze. "Someone carved ivy on our basement wall."

Margaret nodded as if this was a pleasant thing. "Oh yes. We have seen it. Christian did that, Courtney, not long after he carved the ivy on Prudence's gravestone."

"We didn't get a chance to mention it to you yesterday. I'm sorry about that," Mr. Geyer apologized. "Christian actually carved it all over the house—on the walls and the banisters—as if he were carving a trail for Prudence." He glanced in the direction of Prudence's tombstone. "The house burned soon after that. All that was left was the basement."

"Does that make you nervous, Courtney?" Margaret was looking at me with those big green eyes.

"I don't know. Maybe a little." *A trail? A trail leading to what?* "But that's silly," I argued more with myself than anyone. "Prudence died over two hundred fifty years ago."

"Did she?" Margaret asked lightly.

Mr. Geyer shook his finger at her. "Margaret, stop teasing Courtney."

"But we don't have the bones to prove it," she shot back.

"What are you talking about?" I asked, my voice rising. The sane part of me did not want to hear anymore, but the curious part of me yearned for more information.

"Please, Margaret. Don't burden Courtney with our quest."

"But she wants to know!" Margaret objected. "Don't you, Courtney?"

I looked at Mr. Geyer. Little beads of sweat had formed above his upper lip.

"Yes," I whispered. Like it or not, Prudence was a part of my life now. I suddenly noticed how silent the world appeared to be. All I could hear, besides my own beating heart, was the impatient call of a crow.

I turned to Mr. Geyer, who sighed. "Yes. It's true," he admitted sadly. "The cemetery grounds have changed over the centuries. Prudence was originally buried where those cornfields are now." He shielded his eyes with his hand as he looked over at them. "The coffins, of course, were relocated, at least they were supposed to be. But years ago we discovered that whoever was responsible for the move lost Prudence. There was no coffin beneath her tombstone."

"And we think that the ivy is still searching for Prudence," Margaret added excitedly.

"You're kidding." They glanced furtively at each other, and then their gaze settled on me. "You must be!" I insisted. I stared at Mr. Geyer's clown-like eyes. "Whatever made you dig up her grave in the first place?" I asked incredulously.

Mr. Geyer shrugged as he put his arm around Margaret's shoulder. "Well, we didn't exactly dig up her grave. I guess you could say that we dug up the information after Margaret first voiced her suspicions last summer."

"It was the ivy," Margaret interjected. "It reminded me of a mother looking for her lost child."

I'm sure my mouth had dropped open. My forehead was on fire.

"We've already said too much, Margaret. Courtney will think we are crazy." He seemed anxious as he made that pronouncement, looking again from Margaret to me. I got the feeling that he did not want Margaret to lose the chance of having a real friend.

Yep. From the corner of my eye, I could see the ivy on the sides and front of my house, basking in the sun like it owned the place.

"Can I help you look for her?" I heard myself say.

Margaret responded with a big, beautiful smile.

"That would be nice," she agreed.

The three of us were sitting around our kitchen table. I had invited Mr. Geyer and Margaret in for a glass of Dad's iced tea. He made the best, I had promised them, as he allowed the teabags and fresh lemons to steep in boiled water for hours. They sat, their hands folded patiently in front of them, like kindergartners waiting for their cookies and milk. They both looked around the room as if they were familiar with its space.

"Just look at that collection of copper pots and kettles, Margaret," Mr. Geyer instructed, pointing to the assortment that hung from the rafters.

Who are these people? The thought shot unprovoked through my head. *Why do I feel strange in the company of Mr. Geyer and Margaret?* He was older than my dad and a lot weirder. And Margaret was unlike any girl I had ever known. She was beautiful, mysterious, but didn't seem to care about normal things, like talking about boys or going to the movies. She only cared about Prudence. Having them in my kitchen made it feel like a different place. The room was suddenly charged with intrigue.

"How do you look for a coffin?" I asked as I poured the tea, unable to hold back my question. Margaret began swirling the ice in her glass with her finger to make it colder.

"Thank you, Courtney." Mr. Geyer placed a napkin beneath his glass before he replied. "It's like being an historian or a detective." He took a long sip before he continued. "My compliments to your father. This tea is delicious."

"We've done a lot of research, Courtney," Margaret continued for him. Now she was running her finger up and down the outside of the sweating glass. "Dad and I spent hours at Murmur's town hall and library, searching for old property deeds, town records, and newspaper clippings. When pieced together, they're our best clues."

Mr. Geyer was nodding in agreement. "We found information on the gentleman who acquired a portion of the cemetery in the 1880s. The section that is now the cornfield across the street from your house."

"You mean that other people were once buried there, too?" *Mom and Dad sure knew how to pick a house,* I thought, trying to hide my displeasure.

"Yes." Mr. Geyer smiled, like I was a quick study. "The farmer, Tom Pritchard, owned a few hundred acres adjacent to that part of the cemetery. He had three daughters and, when they married, he wanted to subdivide his farm so that there was enough land for all his relations to make a living. He must have loved those girls, wanting to keep them so close." He smiled at Margaret as if he perfectly understood the sentiment.

Margaret ignored him, though. She was staring out the kitchen bay window, watching the vines of ivy swaying in the light breeze. They draped across the windowpanes like a curtain.

"Can we go into the basement?" Margaret asked. Her eyes were wide and bright, like she could see or smell something that excited her.

"Sure." I was more than happy to show them the ivy carvings. I wanted an expert opinion on what the carvings symbolized, and I didn't quite trust Mom or Dad to supply it.

We quickly drained our glasses. Even Mr. Geyer seemed excited about the prospect of seeing the carvings again. I led the way down the basement stairs after switching on the lights, describing again how I had found the carvings behind the rows of boxes.

The musty smell of earth and stone was more pronounced today. I checked the walls by the basement windows to see if any water had leaked in from the rain, but the walls were dry.

"Smells like a crypt," Margaret said without the trace of a smile in her voice. I looked at her nervously. *How does she know what a crypt smells like?*

"It's behind the boxes." I pointed to the top row as Mr. Geyer approached them. "We can pull them away from the wall, if you'd like."

Mr. Geyer gave me that concerned-adult look. His eyebrows arched skeptically above his glasses. "Are you sure your parents won't mind, Courtney? I'm not sure that I would feel comfortable with strangers rummaging through *my* basement."

"You're not strangers," I protested. We had known Mr. Geyer and Margaret for at least a few days, I thought. It felt like weeks, though. "Mom plans to empty all the boxes before school starts anyway. And besides, we're conducting research. Mom *loves* research."

Mr. Geyer smiled, remembering Mom's enthusiasm about the cemetery tours. "All right, but we must be careful and put everything back as we found it."

"Here, Margaret." Mr. Geyer lifted a box from the top row. "Put this along the front wall, away from the window. The heavy boxes should be on the bottom."

"Here. I can help, too," I offered anxiously. Suddenly I felt frantic to reveal the entire wall.

It only took a few minutes to expose the carvings. The natural light from the adjacent basement window threw a gentle spotlight across the face of the wall. I watched as Mr. Geyer and Margaret approached the carvings reverently. They looked like a pair of archaeologists who had just uncovered an Egyptian tomb, but instead of scarabs, the wall swarmed with sculptured ivy.

Mr. Geyer traced one vine with his finger before speaking. His face was only inches away from the wall.

"I don't remember the carvings being this detailed and furious," he said. "Look at this, Margaret. What do you think?"

At first, Margaret stayed unmoved. I noticed that she was trembling ever so slightly when she finally raised a hand to touch a particularly prominent leaf. It seemed three-dimensional, as if Margaret could grasp it. Even its veins were contoured in relation to the wall.

I stepped back. The bits of carving I saw last night were impressions, faint images of what occupied the wall now.

"It looks as if someone carved these again," Margaret whispered as she turned to face Mr. Geyer. Her face was paler than usual. "Who could have done this?"

They both then looked at me.

"I don't know," I blurted out, feeling suddenly defensive. "When I found the ivy last night, I had to get really close to see it." I pictured myself staring at the vines, squinting to see where they led. "But I didn't move the boxes like we did," I added.

Mr. Geyer cocked his head for a moment, as if he were noticing something about me for the first time. His eyes brightened, and then just as quickly went blank as if someone had blown out a candle. "You're probably right. And it's been a while since Margaret and I have seen the carvings. Maybe our memories are playing tricks on us."

Margaret's hands were on her hips, and her chin was raised. "Perhaps the ivy thinks it has found something," she stated.

I looked back to Mr. Geyer to gauge his reaction. He said nothing as he walked back to the wall to stare at it again.

"In the *basement*?" I yelped. "It's not like we're talking about the *real* ivy. It's just a carving," I insisted.

Margaret shrugged. "Dad, I think we should show Courtney our work, since she wants to help us find Prudence."

Mr. Geyer turned away from the carvings. He wrinkled his forehead when he looked at me. "Do you *want* to see our work, Courtney?"

A shiver ran down my spine. "Sure," I said softly. I didn't want the ivy to hear.

I left Dad a message at work and Mom a message on her cell phone. Mr. Geyer insisted that I let them know where I was going, just in case one of them came home before I returned. Of course, all I said was that Margaret invited me over and that she lived off a little dirt road that hooked into the woods just about a quarter mile south of our house. I was surprised that they lived that close to me. Why had they not told me this before?

The afternoon heat slowed our pace as we walked along the grass swale on our side of the road. Today, under the pounding sun, the stalks of corn looked weary, not threatening as they did yesterday. Instead, it was the heat that pricked at our skin instead of slapping wind or stinging rain. After only a few minutes, our shirts were darkened with sweat.

"You'll be surprised at how much cooler it is at our house, Courtney. The woods keep our house in the shade all the time," Mr. Geyer said cheerfully.

I glanced at a white Ford as it slowed cautiously to pass us. An old couple stared at us with big eyes as they crawled by.

"How long have you lived there?" I directed the question to Margaret.

"Ummm, about a year, I think, right, Dad? We're just renting." She bent to pull a tall blade of grass from the ground.

"Oh," I replied. "I guess I thought you always lived here, maybe because of your cemetery tours," I added lamely.

"Well, that's understandable." Mr. Geyer nodded pleasantly. "I'm a historian of sorts, and my job requires me to travel quite a bit. It's hard on Margaret, I fear," he amended gently.

Margaret tossed her head at the suggestion, her two braids whipping at her right shoulder. "It's not hard at all, Dad. I like our work."

"But it must be hard going to lots of different schools, though, isn't it? I'm always a wreck when I have to meet a whole new set of people, even though I look forward to new adventures," I said sympathetically. I searched Margaret's face for the slightest sign of vulnerability. Her serene features did not crack as her big green eyes locked onto my face.

"You met us just fine, Courtney. You never seemed a bit nervous," said Margaret as she surprised me by slipping her arm around my shoulder.

"Here's the road." Mr. Geyer pointed to what looked to me like a hiking path that turned into the woods. He sounded relieved.

"Me first!" Margaret yelled. She waved for me to follow her as she suddenly sprinted up the path. I did just that, running along the serpentine trail as it zigged and zagged among massive pine trees. In less than a minute, we stood in a clearing in front of an old stone house. The yard was composed of tree stumps and ragged grass.

"This is like *Little House on the Prairie*." I sputtered. We both were breathing hard and I smiled at Margaret to let her know that I was kidding. If you ignored the row of open cat food cans that were lined along the front wall of the house—tuna, chicken, meat, and cheese, each with various proportions still remaining—all the house needed was some smoke curling out of the little chimney.

Wild Cats in the Woods? Margaret just laughed. "Come on in. Dad will catch up in a minute." She pulled a key from her back pocket and pushed open the door. I caught a lingering smell of burned logs from the fireplace.

The house was a bit dark. I guessed the sunlight had a tough time penetrating the woods' thick canopy in the summer. Margaret turned on a table lamp by the couch. The first floor, from what I could see, included the living room with the fireplace, a small dining room with a table covered with papers, and a kitchen with just the appliances in the back. The powder room, as my mom would say, was next to the kitchen.

All the walls were paneled with cedar, and the living room was separated from the loft by thick rafters, where I guessed their bedrooms must be. The coffee table, armchairs, and couch—all the furniture, really—reminded me of mountain houses we had rented on summer vacations.

"It's a rental cabin," Margaret affirmed, as if she could read my mind. "Come sit with me at the table," she instructed, pulling out a chair. "I want to show you what we have found about Prudence so far."

I nodded enthusiastically and plopped myself in the chair beside Margaret. I was eager to see what they had discovered.

"Girls!" Mr. Geyer called from the door. "Such energy! Let's just be thankful that it's always cool in here." He paused at the table to survey the materials spread on its surface.

"Do you mind if I show Courtney now, Dad?" Her eyes suddenly softened as if she were pleading with him. Her smile remained.

"No, of course not, honey. You go ahead and I'll get some refreshments." We both watched as he retreated into the kitchen.

"Look at this, Courtney." Her hands were trembling as she held up a yellowed newspaper clipping, which was all that was needed to release a torrent of stories. The article was about the sale of the section of the cemetery where the cornfield is now. There was a picture of the farmer and his three daughters. They each held a basket with flowers and were smiling shyly. The farmer wore overalls and a straw hat and was leaning toward the camera as if he did not trust its eyesight.

There was no stopping Margaret as she dove into the pile of papers. There were more tattered clippings, photo-copies of clippings, and photographs of people all more than one hundred years old. Margaret showed me old maps that divided Murmur into parcels of land with people's names on each parcel. One map had the cemetery as it appeared before it was divided and sold. It must have been thousands of acres wide and it ran all the way to the creek that still runs through downtown Murmur. Our house was even on the map, titled "Cemetery House". I frowned uncomfortably at it.

"How about this, Courtney?" Margaret thrust some black-and-white photos that showed men in long coats carrying coffins to a horse-drawn wagon. Someone had written 1897 in their corners. "See, we do have some proof that they were moved, but we haven't been able to find the document that says where each was moved to."

"Those are from reproductions of glass negatives, Courtney," Mr. Geyer called from the kitchen. Obviously he was standing in there and listening to us.

"Dad, quit interrupting," Margaret ordered. "I must read you this, Courtney. Dad copied it from a page of Christian's journal."

I was suddenly so anxious to know its contents. I wanted to reach out and snatch the paper from Margaret's hand, but instead I sat and politely listened.

Margaret's voice dropped to signify Christian. I felt the goose bumps spring up all over my arms.

The witch stood before my Prudence's grave. She wore a black shawl against the bitter wind. Her hair was black as a crow's wing and was blowing freely about her. Her skin was pale and flawless. Her eyes green as ivy. I told her as much.

"Ivy?" she repeated, grabbing my hands in her own. Her grip was fierce. She bent to trace the ivy I had carved on Prudence's stone.

"This is beautiful," she whispered. "Touch it as I am."

She gently forced me to kneel in the wet grass. When I placed my hand on the carvings, she sprinkled it with a clear, cool liquid. And then she began the incantation.

I couldn't make out many of the words but I did recognize a few— DEATH and GOD and SATAN. She said something about the roots of life, fertility, and salvation. Her final word was PRUDENCE.

She had tears in her eyes as she pulled her shawl tightly about her.

"God bless your love," she said, before turning away from me to walk to the horse she had tied at the gate. I stayed by the grave all that day and night.

For a moment, I did not say a word. Incredibly, I felt as if I might cry.

Margaret nodded at me. "I know. It's heartbreaking, isn't it?"

"Was she really a witch?" I finally asked.

"What is a witch?" Mr. Geyer asked from the kitchen doorway. "Someone with particular talents and perhaps an affinity for nature?" His voice sounded sad. "I don't know. Margaret and I tried to find out who she was, but Christian never called her by name."

"But Margaret thinks she was a witch, don't you, Margaret?" I trusted Margaret's instincts about the ivy. Margaret was the one who believed that it was searching for something. She seemed to believe that the ivy was something more than just another plant.

Margaret looked at me with an appraising smile. "Yes, Courtney, I do. I *sense* something about the ivy. Something that's not natural."

I felt the same cold thrill I had felt in the basement when Mr. Geyer revealed the ivy carvings behind the boxes. The ivy that looked like it had been fed plant food compared with the carvings I had spied the night before. I sensed something, too, and having Margaret affirm my feelings made my blood course cold.

Mr. Geyer frowned. "Just because we don't *understand* something, Margaret, does not make it strange," he said. His voice was suddenly stern, as if Margaret had broken a rule.

"Yes, Dad," Margaret replied, unrepentant. She flashed me a look as if to say as much.

I felt a weird tension between them for the first time, which bothered me because they got along so well. They were *always* together, I realized.

I looked at my watch. "I had better get home to finish the weeding," I announced quietly. "Please let me know how I can help you both with the search." I needed to be a part of this. I felt like I had no choice. I was bound to Prudence—by the house that she had once lived in, by the witch who used potions to try to bring her back to life, by the cemetery that seemed to have a living presence of its own, and by the ivy that I felt was somehow stalking me, too.

"We will." Mr. Geyer's voice had softened. "In the meantime, show the carvings in your basement to your parents and share with them the history of your house."

"I will," I promised as I threw Margaret one last nervous smile before I opened the door.

Deed of Sale

Murmur, Massachusetts, March 3, 1895

Know all men by these present that I,

JACOB X. HENRY,

ACTING AS AGENT FOR THE TOWN BODY OF

MURMUR, MASSACHUSETTS,

have agreed to sell to

THOMAS R. PRITCHARD

THE ONE HUNDRED ACRES

owned by the town of MURMUR, *situated on* HICKORY CREEK ROAD, *north of* HICKORY CREEK, *and adjacent to the* PRITCHARD FARM.

Said Mr. Pritchard is to pay

FIVE THOUSAND DOLLARS

($5,000)

FOR THE ACRES ABOVE DESCRIBED.

Said Mr. Pritchard will also support and will not hasten
THE RELOCATION and PROPER REBURIAL
of the

EIGHTY-FOUR
HUMAN REMAINS

THAT NOW INHABIT THE CEMETERY
AT THIS SAME LOCATION.

chapter 4

I WAS HOLDING THE GARDEN HOSE OVER MY HEAD AS
Mom screeched into the driveway. My face was pounding with the heat, and my back was sore from bending
down over and over again to pull the remaining weeds that
had been given a reprieve by my break. The ivy must be
training them, I thought. Their roots seemed to extend
toward the center of the earth.

"Courtney! Look at you!" Mom yelled as she slammed
the car door. Dad hates when she does that. I almost told
her so since she was looking at me with such a huge smirk.

My clothes were wet, and the water running refresh-
ingly down my arms and legs left streaks of mud like verti-
cal stripes. I was sure dirt was smudged all over my face,
too. I have a hard time remaining dirt free when working
in a garden.

"And my gloves, Courtney! They're soaked!" She
crossed her arms as she leaned against the hood of the car.

I could tell she was feeling a little cocky today. Her hair was pulled back into a ponytail and she was wearing her bright red lipstick.

"They were soaked when I found them behind that azalea bush!" I protested, taking one glove off and tossing it at her. It landed with a wet thud on the roof of the Jeep.

"Hey!" She laughed, walking toward me and gingerly giving me a kiss on the forehead. "I know. I was just testing you." Her startling blue eyes stared into my own. "You did a nice job here, Courtney. Did Dad see it yet?"

"Nope. You beat him home." I peeled off the other wet glove as I surveyed my work. The tiger lilies, mums, and other odd assortments of flowers had breathing room now. At least only the ivy clung to the stone of the house and didn't seem interested in trespassing in the flower bed.

"*Hmm*. Dad sure knows how to pick flower combinations." She smiled, shaking her head. Suddenly she switched gears.

"Courtney, come into the kitchen and clean up. I'll pour you a glass of iced tea. I need to talk to you about the article I'm working on."

Uh-oh. My mother is also known as a writer-activist. She grabbed my hand and propelled me through the front door. The comparable coolness of the house gave me a sudden chill.

She tossed me a dish towel after I washed my hands.

"Courtney, you won't believe what I found out today," she insisted while pouring me a glass. "Dry your hair so you won't catch pneumonia," she added.

"What?" I asked warily. When she got that crazed look in her eyes, I knew that any idea could become a plan.

She pulled out a chair and joined me at the kitchen table. Her back was to the ivy. I scowled at the leaves drooping against the bay windowpanes. The heat must be getting to the ivy, too.

"Don't frown that way. It's unattractive," she admonished me. "Anyway, the editor of *The Murmur Mercury*," she added when she saw my eyebrows shoot up in a question, "asked me to do a story on urban sprawl. Do you know what that is?"

I did not answer right away, as I was still swallowing a giant gulp of tea. "Yes," I finally replied, enduring her impatient stare. "It's when developers build homes far from cities, usually on farmland or other open areas. We learned about it in school last year." I thought about my eighth-grade teacher who was passionate about all things green. "Mr. Clark was a real environmentalist. He and his friend tied themselves to a bulldozer or something one time." My classmates and I thought that Mr. Clark was a nut.

"Good for Mr. Clark!" my mom practically cheered.

"Anyway, I found myself interviewing this developer about the fifty or so homes he hopes to build right outside of Murmur's downtown." She stared at me to draw a reaction.

I could not help but think that at least there would be some more people around here. "Where does he want to build the homes?" I asked to appease her.

"On a portion of the remaining cemetery. It's over two hundred acres. The developer claims that there is no room left for new burials, and he's willing to pay a nice price to relocate the existing remains." She slapped her palm on the table. "No one will care, he insisted. Can you believe that?" Her face was now as red as mine.

I suddenly saw the vines of ivy swaying outside in the wind. I tried to recall even the slightest breeze when I was weeding. *Someone will care . . . a lot.*

We were waiting for Dad on the front steps when he pulled into the driveway in his pickup. The candy-apple-colored pickup was new with the house. Dad said we needed one now that we lived in New England. Mom told me that all little boys want a pickup truck, and if they never get one, it's like dying with an unrequited love

hanging over their heads. Mom gave the pickup a mean stare. Suddenly the truck symbolized builders and the sprawl left in their wake.

"Whoa," Dad said, pulling the truck in front of the steps. "Did I do something *that* serious?" His tie was off and the truck's windows were down. His red hair was standing on end.

"Nice look, Dad," was all I could say before Mom was up and standing by the driver's side door.

"Tom, did you know that there is a developer interested in buying up some of the cemetery and building houses on it?" Her arms were crossed over her chest as if she dared him not to know.

"You're kidding." His tone was serious to match my mom's. His "Mom antennae" were usually well tuned. "Is that the story you were assigned? I got your message at work but it wasn't clear."

Mom nodded. "Yes. We have to figure out how to fight this."

My dad glanced at me to see if I was upset, but I just shrugged.

"Jen, let me park this thing and change out of these clothes and we'll talk. I'll throw some burgers on the grill, okay?" He flashed her his best boyish smile.

"All right," she agreed. She patted him playfully on the

cheek before he pulled around to the "wall of the east wing" of the house to park in the back by the shed.

"Shall we go in and wash up?" she asked, putting her arm around my shoulder. "I hope you don't think your mom is crazy."

"Well," I started jokingly, but I was interrupted by a voice calling from the end of the driveway.

"Courtney! Mrs. O'Brien!" It was Margaret and Mr. Geyer walking along the road toward the cemetery. Brochures were tucked under Mr. Geyer's arm. I had not seen them give one tour yet, I realized.

"Mr. Geyer! Wait!" my mom called, her voice hitting a pitch it only reaches when she's excited. "I must talk to you!"

Mr. Geyer's eyebrows were raised in surprise as my mom jogged down the driveway. I trotted right behind her. Margaret smiled as if truly glad to see us. "Let me hold the brochures for you, Dad," she offered as she slipped them from his side.

My mom looked at Mr. Geyer as if she had hit the lottery. "Forgive me for shouting, but I couldn't let you get away." She laughed. She was just as suddenly serious. "I need to ask you if you know anything about a developer who wants to build homes on parcels of the cemetery, that is, once he purchases the property and relocates the remains."

For a moment, Mr. Geyer said nothing. Margaret glanced at the cemetery and then back at our house.

"We did hear that," Margaret answered for him. The smile was gone from her face.

"Well, we heard the rumors," Mr. Geyer corrected. "We prayed they were not true. This cemetery is precious. It must not be disturbed again." He pronounced this like a church minister addressing his distracted congregants.

My mom seemed captivated by his eyes. They seemed to float behind his lenses, as if disconnected from his body.

"I agree," she finally replied.

"Then we'll need your help," he said. All the humor was gone from his voice. It must have been ninety degrees out, and yet I felt the hair stand up on the back of my neck.

"Well, actually, I have an idea," my mom said, as if challenged. "I'm doing a story on it for our weekly paper, so it would be a conflict of interest for me to get personally involved." Her speech tumbled rapid-fire as it does when she is excited and does not want anyone to interrupt her. "But you know this cemetery better than anyone. If you want to gain attention about its plight, perhaps a protest could be arranged. Then I can cover the story for the paper. You'll need to rally the people of Murmur to fight for its protection."

"That's a wonderful idea," Margaret agreed.

Mr. Geyer turned to my mom and I could almost see his demeanor soften.

"An interesting proposition, Mrs. O'Brien," he agreed, the chill gone from his voice.

"Do you have any ideas?" my mom asked hopefully.

"Perhaps." He nodded, a bit distractedly. "But don't worry. I'll come up with something newsworthy, I promise you."

"Great." My mom beamed. "I'll need to interview you, too, as the cemetery's expert. And I'll want you to start calling me Jenny," she insisted.

"Certainly." Mr. Geyer suddenly seemed very calm.

"Can we pick a time to talk tomorrow? My article is due by Wednesday. Will that give you enough time to brainstorm a plan?"

"It will have to be enough time." Mr. Geyer smiled patiently. "Time waits for no man."

I looked at the cemetery and tried to picture winding tree-lined streets with nice big houses and lots of people. Would it really be that bad? Then I remembered Prudence. *If Prudence was still lost from the first move, how many others might be displaced?*

"Exactly," Margaret said, turning to me, although I am sure that I had not voiced my thoughts out loud.

CHRISTIAN GEYER
STONECUTTER ON HICKORY CREEK ROAD

Hereby informs his Customers and other Gentlemen and Ladies that in addition to conducting stonecutting business as usual, he carries on the Art and Manufactory of many images viz: angels, skeletons, suns, moons, snakes, birds, sheep, the likenesses of the departed, and many intricate designs that include flowering vines, acorns, lilies, and ivy in its intricacy and fullness.

As said Geyer has been at a considerable Expense in making Preparations in order to accomplish said Art, he hopes the Gentleman and Ladies will be so kind as to favour him with their Custom.

chapter 5

M

ARGARET, MR. GEYER, AND I WERE SITTING BY
Prudence's grave. Despite the high August temperatures there was a nice breeze, which made
the sitting bearable. Today Margaret's hair was pulled back
in a single thick braid, taut against her face, making it look
almost shrunken. She had the witch's emerald eyes.

Margaret had brought along another copy from a page
of Christian's journal, to inspire us in planning our cemetery protest.

*The witch stood on my threshold today. She
looked from my raw hands to the ivy that I had
just finished carving on my door. Ivy swirled in
concentric circles between the knocker and knob
as if caught up in the wind.*

*"I saw you from the road," she explained.
Her green eyes seemed to penetrate my soul.*

"She hasn't come home yet," I accused. I was ashamed that she saw me this way. She was a witch, but she was also a woman.

"You must be patient, sir. It's only been a few days. Nature does not heed our hourglass."

"Leave me alone," I begged. "Unless you have another spell that can speed the hands of time."

She shook her head. "No one is that powerful. God would not permit it. We must work within His laws."

I wanted to push her away. I almost raised a hand to her. Her black hair blew in a cloud about her head, as if my thoughts agitated the wind, but she turned away on her own.

"Impatience only breeds fury and fury fire" she warned as she walked back to the road and her horse.

"Why only one page?" I asked. I was hooked. I wanted to hear more.

She was pleased by the question and placed her hand over mine. "I just picked an excerpt that I thought was appropriate for today. I'm afraid of leaving the house with even one. What if it got damaged or lost?" Her face was beseeching. Her question seemed sincere.

I looked at the skeleton head, the bats, the angels, and the ivy decorating Prudence's tombstone and nodded. I understood. Every clue to Prudence's whereabouts was precious.

Mr. Geyer was walking along one of the gravel paths with a notebook, jotting as he paused and peered at various tombstones. Wispy white clouds raked the blue sky behind him. The hearty sycamores and willows that had grown on this land from tiny seeds seemed to stand at attention. Their leaves barely stirred. Mr. Geyer seemed incongruous in this pastoral scene in his jeans and plaid shirt. Then again, he looked out of place wherever he was. I was beginning to recognize his limited wardrobe already.

"It's teasing, isn't it, Courtney?" He glanced at Margaret, who was crouching now and plucking at the weeds daring to sprout around Prudence's plot. "When I found Christian's journal at the historical society, I stayed up all night reading it. I was entranced." His eyes were focused on my face, but when he turned slightly, his glasses appeared like fun-house mirrors. Talk about entrancing. I looked back to Margaret.

"The story is so sad. Even the little bit of it I've heard," I murmured. I wanted to ask to borrow the journal, but an historical society would never trust it with a kid. I would have to wait for the pages that Margaret would share with me.

Margaret stood slowly and began to brush the dirt from her hands. "It is sad, especially because we know how it ends, but I brought this page to get us thinking. Dad said we needed a theme." She brought the page close to her face, as if she missed something.

"How about . . ." she began. "'Impatience only breeds fury and fury fire'?" she suggested.

I wrinkled my nose. "Sounds kind of threatening," I offered. "I don't think we want to scare people." I glanced around us. The cemetery was deserted. Who was there to scare?

Mr. Geyer came up beside me. "I think you're right, Courtney. Perhaps we should think about 'Nature does not heed our hourglass.'"

Now it was Margaret who squinted in doubt. "And what's the message there?" She raised her hand to shield her eyes from the sun.

"That nature has its own schedule, and thus its own design." Mr. Geyer's chin was raised in contemplation as he spoke.

"I think I need to know exactly what we are planning before I can pick a theme," I confessed. A sudden breeze played gently with the ends of my hair. It felt like the affectionate hands of a friend.

"Maybe we should just tell them about Prudence," I blurted. "Her story sure got me hooked."

Margaret and Mr. Geyer both sort of cocked their heads at me.

"Tell them what?" Mr. Geyer asked guardedly. I felt those big eyes of his scrutinizing every inch of my face.

"Uhhh . . ." Suddenly I felt like I was taking a test. "About her missing coffin. How the first time they relocated the cemetery, they lost people's remains to make room for the farm." My voice got stronger as the idea made perfect sense to me. "There may still be people in town who have ancestors buried here. Nobody wants their ancestors going missing." I shrugged when they both continued to stare.

Margaret stood by Prudence's grave and then suddenly crouched, as if waiting to hear Prudence whisper her opinion. Mr. Geyer opened his notebook and began flipping the pages. *What is with these two?* They seemed unconvinced.

"Who knows?" I braved, only slightly daunted by the vexing silence. "Maybe we can get the cemetery registered as an historic site. My teacher at home tried that, but he was a little too nerdy and people wouldn't pay attention to him." I was looking at Mr. Geyer's black socks as I said this.

"Margaret can tell them, and I'll help." People would

listen to Margaret. She at least *looked* normal and was incredibly well spoken. Adults would listen to her. I knew this instinctively.

Margaret stood and reached for my hand. For a girl my age, she had some old-fashioned habits, like this hand-grabbing thing right out of *Little Women*.

"I think that's a terrific idea." Her usually pale face was flushed. She was breathing fast. "We have the photos and the newspaper clippings about the relocation. We just need to show some proof that Prudence is missing."

"What do you mean?" I asked. "I thought you had her grave dug up."

Margaret's green eyes opened wide. "Courtney, we said we dug up some information. We're not allowed to dig up a grave, but perhaps in this case. . . ." she added wistfully. Her gaze darted to Mr. Geyer's face. She gave him a look that said, *Well?*

"Then can we use the information that you already found?" *Well what?* I was confused. *Why is everything such a riddle with them?*

"No, we cannot, Courtney." Mr. Geyer had the same stern look on his face he took on last night with my mother. "The information I have, if published, could compromise my research. And I don't want to mention Christian Geyer or the ivy in any way. Is that understood?"

I must have been squinting at him, as if a complete stranger had suddenly taken over the body of Mr. Geyer. "I don't want to, either," I agreed, thinking of the ivy blazing trails along my basement walls. I probably sounded a bit offended.

"Dad," Margaret interrupted, "Courtney is just trying to help. She has a good idea. We can make this work." Margaret's chin was in the air again.

It was amazing how she can soften him. The notebook dropped to his side and he scratched his head like he was thinking about a long-ago memory. "I'm sorry, Courtney. I care so much about this cemetery that it makes me fierce. I know you are our ally. Forgive my rudeness. I guess I'm feeling the pressure of this fight."

"I understand," I said. And I did. For the past year, this research was their whole life. I turned to measure with my eyes the vast expanse of the cemetery, extending without limit from my vantage point. I tried to imagine houses with big yards and decks suddenly in this place. It *was* jarring. It felt sacrilegious.

I turned back to smile in sympathy at Mr. Geyer and Margaret. I knew what they were feeling, but my smile dissolved as I saw them staring in the direction of my house. Mr. Geyer's brows were raised as if in surprise. Margaret's mouth was slightly open.

"What is it?" I asked nervously. It looked the same to me—an ivy-bound house surrounded by woods and cornfields.

Mr. Geyer rubbed his forehead like he had a headache. "Nothing, Courtney. Just thinking about all the work that still needs to be done."

Margaret and I stood at the end of my driveway and caught the breeze of a passing car before we turned down the road. Mr. Geyer was left behind with my mother. He was probably sitting at the kitchen table now, those pots and pans suspended over his head, as my mom pulled out her yellow tablet for the interview. She liked to write big. Little notebooks were not her style.

I had wanted to sit in on the interview. I knew my mom would ask good questions about the cemetery and Mr. Geyer's role in its protection. Questions that I would never have thought about or dared to ask. Questions only an adult can ask another adult. But then again, my mom had no knowledge of the ivy or Christian's journal, and from what Mr. Geyer had told me in the cemetery just an hour ago, he was not going to tell her.

Margaret and I were quiet as we walked along the bed of the drainage swale. It was already dry and hard, as if the August sun had sucked up all the moisture from the ground. I gazed up at the leafy canopy that periodically shaded our walk. Some of the trees were so large that their thicker branches arced across the road, allowing their shoots to brush softly against the swaying stalks of corn.

"Courtney, my dad didn't mean to be harsh," Margaret said apologetically. She cocked her head, awaiting my reaction. Her green eyes were serious as she used the back of her hand to wipe the perspiration from her forehead. "He's just worried about the cemetery. He knows your idea to teach people about the cemetery is a good one. That's why he sent you and me home to begin working on the posters."

I gave Margaret one of my biggest smiles, the kind I give to Mom and Dad when they are acting like the world is coming to an end. I didn't like Margaret looking pinched with worry. Maybe it was that tight braid of hers.

"I know, Margaret. He was just being single-minded, the way grown-ups can get when they've got a problem," I replied, pulling my damp T-shirt off my skin. I was looking forward to the permanent shade of the woods. I could see the dirt path that led to the Geyers' house about five hundred yards farther down the road.

Margaret emitted a musical little laugh. "Single-minded! That's a very good description of him, Courtney. My dad would be the first to admit it."

"My mom can be, too. Actually, that could be a very good thing for the cemetery—two single-minded champions," I declared proudly. I had recently finished *The Once and Future King* as part of my summer reading list. King Arthur believed that the mighty should protect the weak from evil. *Who more than the dead would need someone fighting their cause for them?* I realized with some excitement that we had a cause now, although I was not sure if we had the might.

"I think we can do it," Margaret said, as if she had read my mind again. She grabbed my arm to pull me toward the dirt path as a car whooshed by, unsettling the wildflowers that grew along the swale. The temperature seemed to drop ten degrees as soon as the odor of pine needles perfumed the air.

We began to walk faster once we were in the woods, propelled by a mixture of excitement and shade.

"Do you have a mailing list of people who have attended your tours? Maybe we can alert them about the cemetery and invite them to our event." Mr. Clark, my eighth-grade teacher, did that when he was fighting to save some land. People actually showed up, but were disappointed to find that the only show was Mr. Clark tied to that bulldozer.

Margaret looked down. "No, we're pretty informal. Our tours are more word of mouth. People don't really sign up." She sounded almost embarrassed.

I was sure if Mr. Geyer told my mom that little tidbit, he would get an earful, but it was not Margaret's fault if Mr. Geyer was not a businessman. I wanted to change the subject for Margaret, even though their little cabin was in view.

"Margaret, do you play soccer or volleyball? I plan to go out for the teams. Maybe we can do it together."

Margaret gave me an odd smile. "I don't get involved much at school, Courtney. I'm not really that popular."

"So what?" I answered, surprised and angry for her. "You and I are friends now. And *I* don't know anyone. We can learn the ropes together."

She stopped as we reached the front door to inspect the row of cat food tins. Most were empty. "That's real nice of you, Courtney, but I have a feeling that whatever happens to the cemetery will kind of decide where I'll be in a few weeks." She looked toward the thick thatch of trees as if searching for her cats. She sounded far away.

"What do you mean?" I asked, truly concerned, but she acted as if she did not hear me as she took a key from her shorts' back pocket and opened the front door.

"Okay, we've got our work cut out for us. Let me grab us both a drink and we can start sorting photos on the dining room table." Margaret was suddenly all business. I had seen that gleam in her eyes before, when we were in my basement, looking at the ivy.

Was Margaret trying to say that they might move away? I'll bring this up later, I promised myself. Friends were allowed to ask those sorts of questions.

I pulled out a chair and slid it close to the dining room table, which was already covered by neat piles of black-and-white photographs. Before I reached for them, I took a quick glance around the house to see if anything had changed since my last visit. The way Margaret was talking, I almost expected to see the Geyers' bags packed and lined up by the door, but there was no luggage announcing an imminent departure. Nothing had changed. The rooms were still mountain-cabin dark and the living room's armchairs and couch were all still angled as they were yesterday. Why did I expect something different? We don't normally move around our furniture. Why would Margaret and Mr. Geyer? But something about them made me feel that nothing should be taken for granted.

I could hear Margaret in the kitchen emptying the ice tray. I started to reach for one of the piles of photographs when I noticed the black-covered book on top of a pile of papers to my right. My stomach did a little flip as I slowly reached for it. My fingers tingled as I lifted it and placed it gently in front of me. I opened it, treating the cover and the yellowed papers between it as fragile as butterfly wings. It smelled like dust as I squinted at the scratchy writing that blackened the pages. The script seemed foreign at first with its alien characters, but if I concentrated I could begin to make out the words. I nearly cried out when I recognized Prudence's name.

"Courtney, I'm sorry, but you can't look at that." I hadn't heard Margaret enter from the kitchen. She smiled apologetically as she picked up the book and placed it back on the pile of papers. "Dad is really fussy about anyone handling Christian's journal. *I'm* not even allowed to look at it unless Dad is in the room."

"I'm sorry, Margaret. I didn't mean to be rude." I could almost see my mother looking over Margaret's shoulder, mortified by my lack of manners.

"Courtney, it's no big deal. Really. It's my fault. I'm the one who's been reading the journal pages to you." Margaret sat down and slid the glass of ice water to me. The cubes floated like a slowly spinning nebula. "It's just that Dad gets really nervous about its age. That's not the original binding," she noted, nodding toward the book. "But the pages are authentic and they're obviously falling apart a little more every time the book is opened."

"Can't your dad take them to somebody who knows how to protect old books?" I asked, appalled at the idea of Christian's life crumbling beneath Mr. Geyer's fingers.

Margaret almost rolled her eyes. "Maybe when he is finished with the transcribing. In the meantime, he won't let that journal out of this house."

I understood. I probably would not want to let it go, either. We spread out the collection of tombstone photos. There must have been at least one hundred of them, and Margaret and I were to choose the ones with the most interesting art and names. These would make for a really depressing photo album, I thought, except for maybe on Halloween.

At least two hours had passed while we whittled our selection down to twenty photos to cover the two posters. We had tombstones with hourglasses, skulls, bats, angels, suns, and moons—but no ivy. We chose stones that belonged to little children—one stone had four different babies' names crammed onto it, each one dying one year after another. Stones that belonged to mothers who died young or young men drowned at sea. We tried to pick the tombstones that would bring tears to your eyes as you imagined the lives of these people. It suddenly struck me that cemeteries were jam-packed with life.

"I never looked at cemeteries that way," Margaret replied pensively. I had not realized that I said it aloud. She looked up, her green eyes clear, despite the images of death splayed beneath her hands. Her appreciative smile softened the determination that usually sharpened her features. "I think we've picked the best photos. Could you get the poster boards, Courtney? They're in the living room, by the front door window."

"Sure," I replied. "We're going to stop this development, Margaret," I announced as I stood. This afternoon, I could be fighting for Margaret—fighting to keep her in Murmur.

I was forcing myself to be hopeful about our media event. It had to work. Besides, we had lots of real fascinating information to share, and with Mr. Geyer telling the story in that dramatic way of his, people would be hooked. I looked out the window as I grabbed the boards, hoping to catch a glimpse of one of the many feral cats that the Geyers kept well fed, but what I saw running toward the line of trees was not a cat but a woman.

I was speechless as I watched her dart across the yard toward the woods. She may have been standing outside this very window until I approached.

The woman was not dressed for a steamy August day.

She was wearing a long black skirt and blouse with long sleeves. A black cloak flapped erratically with her steps. Her long black hair was loose and fell below her shoulders. I thought of Christian's journal and of the witch whose hair was black as a crow's wing.

"Margaret," I squeaked. I couldn't seem to raise my voice.

"Courtney, what is it?" Margaret replied. Her voice sounded far away.

The woman seemed to hear me. She stopped, turned, and looked at me or at the house. She seemed unafraid. As a matter of fact, she raised her chin in the air just as Margaret does when she feels challenged. Even from my post at the window, I could see that the woman was young, with incredibly pale skin, like Margaret's, and the same piercing green eyes. She was beautiful.

She nodded and was gone.

"Margaret!" I screamed. My volume was back. "Did you see her? She's running into the woods!" I wasn't thinking. I just grabbed the doorknob, flung open the front door, and sprinted to the end of the dirt path. I swear I saw the flap of a cape.

"Courtney!" Margaret yelled from the door. "Please don't chase her. Please come back!" I did not realize it then. There was fear in Margaret's voice, but I was unable stop myself.

It was much darker in the woods, I realized, as I felt the sting of the pebbles kicked up in my wake. My heart was beating so hard that I could have been running the hundred-yard dash. Strips of sunlight would momentarily blind me as I squinted down the length of the path to find her. I ignored the overgrown weeds that slapped against my legs and face.

"Courtney." I heard Margaret's cry far behind me as I stopped to get my breath and bearings. The path forked. Both dirt paths looked identical. I could not find any sign of the woman.

Then I heard a horse's whinny toward the left.

"Wait!" I yelled as I charged the path. "Wait?" I berated myself. Like someone running away from me was going to stop because I yelled at them?

This path had a globe of light at its end, as if it led to a clearing or meadow. I reached it in seconds and staggered against the blinding sun. I used both hands to shield my eyes and I searched for her. I heard another whinny to my right, on the fringe of the meadow. I looked just in time to see her effortlessly mount a large black horse. She flicked its reins and galloped toward a path that was invisible to me. She rode toward the east—toward the cemetery and my house.

Q. How long have you lived in Murmur?

A. Margaret and I have been in Murmur for some time although we can put down roots wherever we have found a welcoming environment.

Q. How did you get involved in the protection of Murmur's historic cemetery?

A. We have family buried in the cemetery. Personal connections to something, as you well know, can create powerful ties between people and places.

Q. Do you have family still in the area ~~(what about Margaret's mother?)~~

A. No living family. Only those who are a part of Murmur's rich past.

—Jennifer O'Brien

chapter 6

I WAS UNABLE TO FALL ASLEEP LAST NIGHT. I COULD NOT get the witch out of my mind. She had to be Christian Geyer's witch. I was sure of it. *Who or what else could she possibly be?*

I felt bad I ran yesterday, without so much as a good-bye to Margaret, but after seeing the witch ride off on her black horse toward the cemetery I had to get home. It was almost as if she were *leading* me there. She had looked right at me and sort of cocked her head the way I had seen dog owners pose after they tossed a stick.

Margaret had looked upset when I passed their house. She was still standing in the doorway, where I had left her, when I ran off to pursue the witch. Her eyes were wide as she held one hand to her mouth. She did not say anything or try to stop me, but I swore I could still hear her voice cut through me as if she were yelling my name. I hit the drainage swale alongside the road without looking back.

Of course, when I burst through our front door, my mom was full of questions. She was still in that state of nervous excitement that possesses her when she conducts an interview. Her yellow interview tablet was still in her hand, as if I was to be her next subject. She was standing near the kitchen table where she and Mr. Geyer had talked over iced tea. I thought of the look on his face, when I nearly knocked him into the dirt as I passed him on the road during my mad charge home. He did not look surprised. He looked worried, but he did not say a word to me.

We were at the kitchen table now, both of us with a mug of coffee in our hands, despite the heat. The air conditioner humming mindlessly in the background made it feasible. My mother hated that I already loved the stuff because she was the one who let me have my first "tastes."

Now she was going over the same twenty questions she had launched at me last night.

"Why didn't you tell me about the ivy in the basement?" she started incredulously.

"I guess I forgot," I had said meekly last night, but with

real annoyance this morning. Funny what the sun will do for you.

She leaned a little closer to me, a lock of her blond hair sweeping across an eyebrow. She pursed her lips in doubt.

"Courtney, did you know that Margaret missed a lot of school last year because she was out sick?" Mom asked.

I felt a terrible twinge of guilt. *Out sick?* Margaret was pale but never looked sick to me. "Well, she sort of told me that she wasn't very popular at school. Maybe it was because she missed so much time. . . ." I trailed off. I felt that I was betraying her confidence. I took another gulp of coffee to avoid the discussion.

Mom sighed and pulled her yellow tablet toward her. She glanced at the neat script that expertly filled every line. So unlike the crazed handwriting of Christian Geyer.

"They seem very nice, Courtney," she started cautiously. "But there is something very strange about them. I can't quite put my finger on it." She paused to give me a chance to intervene, but I stared out the window, at the shiny bellies of the ivy leaves that flickered against the glass with the breeze.

"In some ways, he seems very old," she continued. "His mannerisms, a slip of a phrase, even the way he dresses. He looks as if he's stepped right out of the nineteen fifties, so I guess I expect him to be . . . much older than he appears."

Suddenly I exploded. "Oh please, Mom! You're so crit-
ical!" I did not know why she was making me feel angry.
I had thought the same things about Mr. Geyer, but I was
upset. I did not want *her* saying those things.

She was sitting back in her chair. "Courtney! What's
the matter with you? Ever since you came home last night
you've barely said two words. Out with it!"

I tried to put on my calm face, the face that would say
to her: *Why are you screaming at me?*

"Courtney," she almost growled in response.

I wanted to tell her, but I could not. I saw the witch
and was afraid because I did not know what it meant for
me to see her. I did not dare go into the basement until
I talked to Mr. Geyer and Margaret. I realized now that I
needed to make them explain to me what was going on.

The microwave dinged and we both jumped. She had
been defrosting some bagels.

"Courtney, is it the cemetery that is bothering you?
Would you prefer that I don't cover this story?" She reached
across the table now to grab my hand, just to make sure that
I was paying attention. "Your dad and I talked last night,
after I showed him the ivy carvings in the basement. He
thinks we're both getting carried away with our cemetery
crusade, especially if it starts making us believe in ghosts and
old town legends."

Had Dad seen me at my window last night, squinting at the cemetery as if I could see the witch dancing around Prudence's grave? I did expect to see the witch doing something in the cemetery, maybe throwing some more of her potions on the tombstones or carving her own ivy in the bark of a tree. I stayed by the window most of the night watching for her.

"No!" I protested. "I *want* you to work on the cemetery article and Mr. Geyer's interview. I want to work with the Geyers, too, to save . . ." *To save what?* my own thoughts interrupted me. *To save Margaret from moving again? To save Christian and Prudence from the witch? To save the cemetery from development? Yes. All of those things.*

She leaned closer to me, peering at my face. "Courtney, if all this excitement is scaring you in some way. . . ." She glanced at the basement door. "You know, when Mr. Geyer showed me that ivy down there, it gave me goose bumps. Not because I was scared, but because I sensed I was in the presence of something odd and mysterious," she finished. "Your dad thought it was amazing, too, but I think he was more in awe of the craftsmanship. He kept run ning his fingers over the vines, wondering just how they were done."

The idea of Dad's hands touching the ivy made me pause. *Would Christian, or the ivy, mind?* Mom and Dad were both fine. Maybe the carvings were really just that—carvings done by a heartbroken Christian not knowing what else to do with his pain.

Talking to Mom did make me feel better. There were no answers, but I did not feel so alone.

"Mom, I want to save the cemetery. I'm not going to get weird about anything, really." *Would saying this make it come true?*

She smiled, a smile full of conspiracy. "Are you sure that this cemetery event Mr. Geyer is planning isn't bothering you?" When I nodded, she did the same. "Okay, but you must promise me that if your . . . or my . . . imagination gets us creeped out for some reason, you will tell me immediately. Agreed?"

"Yes, I promise," I replied, pushing the witch from my memory for the moment. It would not last long.

After Mom went upstairs to change, she circled back to the kitchen and plopped her briefcase onto the kitchen counter. With great ceremony, she placed her printed copy and disk in a folder.

"Okay, Courtney," she said briskly. "Let's hope this article does what we want it to do—nudge people to care about the cemetery or, at the very least, make them feel a little curious."

I nodded agreeably. "Why can't you e-mail the article to the editor?" I was not in a hurry to see Mom leave.

"The editor wants to review it with me. Computers and Internet systems aren't the most reliable with local weekly newspapers. The paper comes out on Friday and noon today is the submission deadline." She gave me a wistful smile. "I shouldn't be long," she promised, kissing me on the cheek. But in a moment she was back, holding a large brown envelope in her hand. "It's from the Geyers. Addressed to you."

It took every effort in my body to keep me from jumping up and snatching it. I thought of Margaret and the sympathy in her eyes as she placed Christian's journal just beyond my reach.

"Thanks, Mom. I'll finish my breakfast first."

She smiled as if she was glad that I was unruffled by the delivery, but as soon as I heard the front door close and the Jeep's ignition turn, I jumped up and grabbed the envelope. I was careful about opening it, not wanting to tear anything. A little note on white loose-leaf paper was clipped to the top.

Courtney,

Hi. Hope you are not mad. Dad said I could share these pages from Christian's journal with you. He said it would help explain.

Dad and I plan to go into town tomorrow to post some flyers about Saturday. If you want to help, meet us at the cemetery entrance at nine o'clock.

I will understand if you do not want to.

Margaret

"Of course I will be there," I said out loud as I lay Margaret's note carefully aside. There were only three excerpts from Christian's journal, I noticed, a bit disappointed. I recognized Margaret's neat script as I pictured her copying these pages painstakingly from Christian's journal by candlelight. *Candlelight?* Maybe my imagination was getting the best of me.

I looked around the kitchen. The house was completely silent, with the exception of the incessant whir of the air conditioner. My hands were trembling as I picked up the papers. I swear, the house could have burned down all around me, and I would not have noticed as long as those copied pages from Christian's journal were in my hand.

I felt myself flush as I began to read the first entry.

The witch. She keeps coming back. This morning I found her standing beside the woodpile, her horse tied to my fence. Yesterday, she stood brazenly on the road, ignoring the wagons and coaches that passed to and from the cemetery, kicking cold dust at her back. She knew I was peering at her from behind the shutters. She smiled each time. She made me feel like an idiot.

She knew I was afraid to go out. She coaxed me with her bewitching smile. I was sure she knew something about Prudence—something I did not want to hear.

I instinctively looked over my shoulder, out the window and past the clinging ivy, to see if Christian's witch happened to be standing beside our shed. Of course the yard was empty. I greedily took up the second entry.

The ivy is all I have now. When I wake in the morning, I use it to guide me down the stairs. Each leaf in the banister reminds me that I am alive as I feel the smooth and sharp grooves of the wood where I gouged the ivy to life. The ivy on my walls is a covenant—an unbreakable bond between Prudence and myself. I placed both hands on this ivy when I heard the rap at the door.

It was the witch.

"Sir, I am concerned about you." Her gaze took in my walls and stopped at my banister. "I didn't mean for this to happen," she said. It was the first time she ever turned away from my stare.

"Prudence has not come home yet," I reminded her bitterly, "You are no witch."

Now she turned back to me, a flash of hell in her eyes.

"Oh, but I am. I came to offer you an eternal bond."

Her voice was strange. Not at all like a woman's. I tried to close the door but her black boot held it in place.

"If you truly love your Prudence, you will let me in."

"There is nothing more you can do," I argued. She had already turned me into a recluse—a man who lived best with the dead.

Suddenly she grasped my hands and turned them gently in her own to reveal my callused palms. There was a new softness in her green eyes as she caressed my hands with her own.

"What are you doing?" I demanded. She was more frightening in her mildness.

"Do you believe in the spirit? Do you believe that one's essence, made of their love and hate and desire, is so powerful that it lives on long after the body is eaten by worms?"

I looked at her uncomprehendingly.

"You must believe," she insisted. "The very air we breathe is seething with the passions of all of those who have passed before us. The dead are not in their graves. Only their bones reside there. The dead make up our elements. They fuel the wind, fire, and water forces that churn our world. I can harness this force for you to ensure that you and Prudence are forever bound."

"Leave me alone," I begged. The witch was tempting me beyond my sanity.

I was not ready to read the final excerpt. This last one had set my heart pounding. What did she mean that the dead are not in their graves? That their essence lives forever? Spirits going to heaven is one thing, but spirits hanging around the earth?

I looked at the ivy on the window, a dull green in the brilliant morning sunlight. *Are those leaves staring at me? Ridiculous.* Just because they seem to be hanging so attentively from their vines. What else were they supposed to do? Suddenly I wished Mom was home.

I looked at the paper in my hand—Christian's nightmarish thoughts in Margaret's careful script. He sounded scared, and *he* was an adult. He didn't have to listen to the witch. I moved the third journal entry to the top of my thin pile. Would this one tell me just how desperate Christian really was?

Each morning I found her standing in a different spot—by the privy, the woodpile, the wall, or the road. It was as if she were tracing a charmed circle around my house with her presence. On the eighth morning, she stood outside my door.

I wouldn't fight her anymore. The cold air was meaningless against my chilled bones.

"Are you ready, sir?" she asked tenderly. Today she spoke like a woman.

"I am," I replied. My voice already had the tone of the dead.

She pulled a few tendrils of fresh ivy from her cloak. It was February, but I did not ask her of the ivy's origin.

"This has become your symbol—the symbol of your love for Prudence. Tonight you must burn this ivy and sprinkle its ashes about your bed. Its essence must become a part of your earthly prayers and must be inhaled with the breath of your dreams."

She placed the ivy in my hands and closed my fists around it. Then she began her incantations—a slow whine that ended like the screech of death. This time I did not recognize any of the words.

"What did you say?" I asked. She was shaking, as if possessed, but her smile was serene.

"Your search for Prudence will reach over the centuries—will be a seed of desire in all of those who come after you, until you and Prudence are united."

NO POSTING
ORDINANCE:
PROHIBITED CONDUCT.

Flyers, circulars, posters, and
other signage may not be mounted on:

(1) Utility poles;

(2) Streetlights;

(3) Traffic or parking signs or devices,
including any post to which such sign
or device is attached;

(4) Historical markers; or

(5) City-owned trees or trees
in the public right-of-way.

—*Murmur Chamber of Commerce Beautification
Committee, as adopted by City Ordinance*

chapter 7

I SAT IN THE GRASS IN FRONT OF THE CEMETERY ENTRANCE, *Memento Mori* above my head like a banner. *As if somebody living next to a cemetery could actually forget death*, I thought peevishly. I was a half hour early for my rendezvous with the Geyers, but I wanted to make sure that I did not miss them. I had so much to ask.

I leaned my back against the iron posts of the fence with the envelope in my hand. I knew I had to give it back to them for safekeeping. We were sort of our own little team now in our quest to help the Geyers and the cemetery.

I glanced down the road and saw Dad's red pickup truck cruising slowly in my direction. A blue car that was idling behind him beeped as Dad turned left to pull into the apron of the cemetery entrance. He frowned as he muttered, "I had my turn signal on. Road rage is supposed to be a city phenomenon."

He switched emotional gears when he turned his attention back to me. "Courtney, are you okay? You bolted past Mom and me at breakfast and you were so quiet during dinner last night." He scrunched his freckled nose in concern. "You even agreed to do all the weeding in the back of the house without so much as a dirty look." He sounded playful but I could detect the caution in his voice.

"Dad, I'm fine, really. Planning this cemetery protest is a great service project for school, don't you think?" I smiled brightly at him. He squinted at me. Obviously he did not buy it.

"Courtney, I know you and Mom are really excited about this, and it is a good thing that you're fighting to preserve the history of Murmur." He glanced at *Memento Mori*. "It's just that you seem sort of preoccupied or worried about something."

"I *am* worried, Dad. What if we lose our fight for the cemetery?" My reaction this time was genuine.

We both seemed to lift our heads as if to welcome the gentle breeze. It smelled of the cornstalks that it tickled. "Courtney, it's the fact that you're fighting a battle that you believe in that's important. Not whether you win or lose, okay?"

I nodded. "Yeah, I know. But I want to win." I *needed*

to win, I thought—for Margaret, for Mr. Geyer, and for Prudence. I was unsure whose side the witch was on.

Dad suddenly grinned. "With Mom fighting on your side, you should come out on top." He peeked at his watch. Watch checking every five minutes was wired into his being. "Okay. I have got to go. Get up and give me a kiss," he demanded teasingly.

I jumped up and kissed him good-bye on the cheek. It was smooth and smelled of his lime aftershave.

"Love you, sweetie. See you at dinner."

I waved as I watched him drive down the road toward Murmur. What could I tell Dad? We could probably use at least one practical guy in this battle.

"Courtney!"

I turned to see Margaret waving enthusiastically as she and Mr. Geyer walked along the swale. She sounded excited and relieved to see me. Today she was wearing shorts and a red tank top, and her hair was pulled back in a loose ponytail. She looked great. Mr. Geyer was wearing another pair of his seemingly endless supply of old-man plaid shorts and a black shirt and socks. His glasses glinted in the morning sunlight. A black backpack hung loosely from one shoulder, bouncing lightly as he walked. This morning I did not wince at the spectacle, I was so glad to see him.

When they were only a few yards from the cemetery entrance, Margaret ran up and hugged me. I was surprised by the fierceness in her voice.

"I'm so glad that you're here, Courtney, and that you are all right." She pulled away to fix her probing green eyes on mine.

A shiver of panic ran through me. *All right? Did she think that the witch would hurt me?*

"Of course I'm okay." I brushed my own fear away with a false bravado. I was a little embarrassed by my behavior in the woods.

I turned to Margaret and offered her the envelope. "I wanted to give this back to you. Mom would have loved to have gotten her hands on it." I laughed.

Margaret smiled knowingly. "So that's where you get your inquisitive nature," she added impishly.

"Did these help you at all, Courtney?" Mr. Geyer asked, still serious.

"A little bit, I think," I answered honestly. "But do you mind if I ask you a few questions?" I asked softly. Margaret was searching my face with those wide green eyes. I was nervously fingering the hem of my shirt.

"Of course," Mr. Geyer replied. He was looking into the cemetery now, as if he was assessing the kingdom of monuments that we were fighting to protect.

"Did the witch put a spell on Christian that was passed on to you?" I whispered, afraid to ask the question in a normal voice.

Mr. Geyer nodded. His larger-than-life eyes, forever trapped behind those lenses, were moist. "Yes, and on to Margaret, too. Although Christian did not have direct descendants, all who share his bloodline are touched by this spell."

My heart picked up speed. "How can you break the spell, then?" All spells could be broken, I thought.

Mr. Geyer smiled sadly, then visibly sagged. Margaret grabbed her father's hand.

"We have to find the remains of Prudence and Christian and reunite them," she said almost matter-of-factly, as if it were the most perfectly normal thing in the world.

"Christian?" I echoed. I had never even wondered about Christian's burial place. "You mean he's not in this cemetery?"

Mr. Geyer and Margaret shook their heads. "No. There is no record of his death. We've been searching a number of known family plots for years, without any luck."

Another thought struck me. Again I was jolted that I had never questioned this before. "What about Prudence's mother?"

Mr. Geyer sighed before answering. "We don't know

anything about Prudence's mother. Record keeping back then was not quite as good as it is today," he added wistfully.

"Christian never even mentioned her in his journal?" I asked, incredulous.

"No," he replied soberly. "It doesn't make sense, does it?"

I stared into the cemetery. Christian had spent a good deal of his life carving memorials for people who died before him. Remembering was his job. How could he neglect to make sure that Prudence's mother would not be forgotten or that his own resting place would be known to his descendants? Was it because of the spell and the witch?

"What about the witch?" I asked boldly, ignoring my instinct that I was pushing all bounds of decency. Each of my questions seemed to knock Mr. Geyer in the gut.

Margaret's grip on her father's hands tightened. Mr. Geyer patted her arm reassuringly. *Is Margaret afraid of the witch?*

"We don't know much about the witch, Courtney, except from what we have gleaned from Christian's journal." He pulled Margaret closer to him and gave her a gentle hug. "Neither of us has ever seen her, although she makes her presence known to us from time to time."

My jaw must have dropped.

"Then why did I see her?" I asked, fighting goose

bumps despite the early-morning heat.

"We don't know, Courtney, but I prefer to take her appearance as a good sign."

Margaret looked at him, a question in her eyes. I looked at Margaret, searching for some reassurance. She reached out and grasped my hand.

"Perhaps because you are not a member of our family." She smiled, as if this reason alone should provide me with comfort.

We took the jitney, as Mr. Geyer called it, into Murmur. Although its seats had lost their spring and the true color of its interior had long ago faded, it was air-conditioned. A few older women with cloth shopping bags clutched against their laps sat in the front. Probably to better position themselves to be the first into their targeted stores. The three of us were fairly quiet as we bounced our way into town. I could not stop thinking about the witch and about what Margaret had said. *Why wouldn't the witch want to appear to Christian's family? Wouldn't she feel closest to them?* But when I had opened my mouth to ask Margaret about it, Mr. Geyer shook his head just enough for me to see. *Not now*, his eyes had beseeched, seeming to float confoundedly behind his glasses.

Murmur was already familiar to me, thanks to my trips to the grocery store and library with my mom. We passed more farms, thatched with cornstalks and some other long, brown, wavy crop that I could not identify.

"Wheat," Margaret said into the air. She was staring out the window, as if hypnotized by the fields that flowed into the horizon.

I was beginning to believe that she *could* read my mind.

The landscape began to change as we approached Murmur. The road suddenly began to gently weave and dip between the thick maple trees and homes that resembled farmhouses but without the farms. Instead most of the homes were surrounded by bushy, trimmed hedges thicker than walls.

Plain stone churches anchored a number of corners, with their glassed-in announcement boards blaring daily reminders to passersby. *Now is the Time. Believe and you will touch Heaven.* It was nice to think that life could be so simple. I bet these ministers never had to deal with missing remains and witches.

The jitney slowed as it turned onto Main Street. It pulled to a stop in front of the post office, its door swishing open to introduce the noises of the little town—horns beeping, people laughing, and a church bell ringing. I could hear the sound of locusts in the trees, invisible but obviously numbering in the millions. At home, the cicadas were our one-instrument orchestra.

"This is the corner," Mr. Geyer announced. The shopping ladies did not even glance our way as they clogged the exit of the jitney. We thanked the driver, and he gave me a friendly nod.

We crowded around the mailbox as Mr. Geyer unzipped his backpack and removed a folder. He gently unclipped the stack of flyers.

"Well, what do you think?" he asked proudly.

Margaret and I stared at the paper. It read:

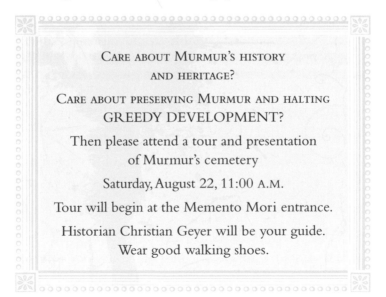

CARE ABOUT MURMUR'S HISTORY
AND HERITAGE?

CARE ABOUT PRESERVING MURMUR AND HALTING
GREEDY DEVELOPMENT?

Then please attend a tour and presentation
of Murmur's cemetery

Saturday, August 22, 11:00 A.M.

Tour will begin at the Memento Mori entrance.

Historian Christian Geyer will be your guide.
Wear good walking shoes.

A photo of the cemetery's *Memento Mori* entrance graced the top of the page.

"Do you think it says enough?" I asked. I knew nothing about putting a flyer together.

Margaret's eyebrows were scrunched in study. "I like the photograph," she said.

Mr. Geyer laughed. "I'll have you know, Courtney, that I worked on this text with your mother. She told me to keep it short and simple, particularly since her article will appear in tomorrow's newspaper."

I smiled. I should have known Mom would have had a hand in this.

"Here, let me give you each a short pile. We'll split up, going up and down these few blocks to post them."

Margaret and I each extended our hands as if we were receiving a gift. It was then that I noticed a number of people eyeing me curiously as they entered and exited the post office. Maybe they were already wondering what the flyers were all about. Good. I pressed them against my chest as if they were a secret.

"I'll begin at this corner," Mr. Geyer directed as he pulled three small rolls of masking tape from his backpack. "Courtney, why don't you start across the street at the coffee shop? They have a community bulletin board in there. Margaret, you head on over to the next block.

Try the realty office and the library. Only hang them on bulletin boards. Telephone poles are not an option in Murmur."

I was excited as I crossed the street. I felt like I was doing something tangible to save the cemetery. As I entered the coffee shop, the aroma of hazelnut pinched my nose. I was surprised to see that the little tables and chairs were filled. Judging from their clothes, they were tourists and businesspeople. I quickly pinned a flyer smack-dab in the middle of the board.

"Cool! Why don't you leave one at each table?" the young guy behind the counter asked. He was looking at the photo on the flyer. I looked at his Grateful Dead T-shirt.

"Sure," I replied in my friendliest voice. Every person helps.

Outside the coffee shop, I stood for a moment to select my next target. I smiled as I watched Mr. Geyer exiting the post office, a small stack of flyers draped over his arm. He gave me an encouraging wave, but there was something strange about him, stranger than usual.

I kept staring at him as he walked down the sidewalk toward the grocery store. He dropped his tape. As he bent down to pick it up, a guy walking in the other direction nearly walked right on top of him. The guy didn't slow down or even look back to apologize to Mr. Geyer. Mr. Geyer seemed unfazed.

I looked down the street for Margaret and spotted her on the library's little bulge of a hill in front of the community board pillared into the ground. I noticed she was careful to avoid the yellow chrysanthemums that shone like tiny suns around the bases of the sign's two posts. Two girls, in halter tops and jeans with summer reading books in their hands, were talking practically a foot away from Margaret. They didn't even sneak a look at her or pause to check out the notice that she was pinning to the board. It was positively abnormal. Girls *always* scrutinize a strange girl in their midst.

I found myself running toward her, my stack of flyers flapping in the wind as I dodged moms with baby strollers, little kids with bikes, and mobs of teenagers hanging out on the front steps of the stores or leaning against parking meters. One year in track, I ran the hurdles, but they were never the human variety. People were giving me dirty looks or yanking little kids aside when I *almost* jostled them. A Volkswagen Beetle sounded its horn as I jaywalked across the street, but I knew they could see me.

Margaret was on the corner now, standing next to the traffic light, where a family in polo shirts stood pushing the button to change the light. She smiled at me.

"Courtney, what are you doing? You ran down that block as if you were practicing the hurdles! You didn't tell me you wanted to go out for track, too." Was I really that easy to read? Her eyes were bright and she was truly enjoying herself. I didn't want to crush her good spirits, but I had to know. I grabbed her by the wrist, pressing hard to feel her bones.

"Ouch," she blurted out, pulling back. "Courtney?" she then asked, her green eyes saucered with alarm as I held tight to her wrist.

"The people here . . . they don't seem to see you," I stuttered.

She glanced at the people passing us on both sides of the sidewalk, as if she had just noticed that indeed there were people here.

"Of course they see us," she replied, her no-nonsense demeanor kicking right in. "They're just used to seeing Dad and me with our cemetery flyers. Let me show you," she said, prying my fingers from her wrist.

Before I could reach out to grab her again, she suddenly stepped off the curb and stood in the path of a red SUV that slowed to round the corner. The car screeched dramatically to a halt. People everywhere stopped to stare at *me*.

"See?" She smiled, vindicated. She didn't even look at the car whose fender was poised only twenty inches from her knees. Over her head, I could see Mr. Geyer standing on the opposite corner, clutching his flyers to his chest.

"Are you crazy?!" I yelled. "You didn't have to do that!"

"But I did," she replied, earnest again. "I don't want to lose your friendship, Courtney. Most friends don't have a good time posting cemetery flyers." She lifted her chin as if daring me to refute that.

As she stepped back onto the sidewalk, I heard the driver of the SUV, a guy about my dad's age, swear as he mumbled, "I didn't get a good look at the person. He was just a blur."

THE MURMUR MERCURY

Homes and Gardens Section   APRIL 13, 1982

English Ivy Is Beautiful and Mysterious

The symbolism of the ivy rests on three facts: It clings; it thrives; and it is an evergreen. Its ability to hold on to stone walls, buildings, and trees, and cover them completely lends ivy its image of resilience, as it "clings" to the things it loves. It also represents faithfulness and undying affection. As an evergreen, the ivy also symbolizes eternal life and resurrection. Medieval Christians, noticing that ivy thrived on dead trees, used it to symbolize the immortal soul, which lived even though the body (represented by the dead tree) decayed.

Editor's Note: English ivy is an invasive plant and should be planted with care.

chapter 8

THE JITNEY RIDE HOME HAD BEEN QUIET, AS IF THE
earlier enthusiasm and joy we had felt was thwarted
by what seemed a new worry in each of us. I
thought about Margaret and Mr. Geyer. *Why wouldn't the
people in town look at them?* Sure, they may have posted lots
of flyers over the past year, and people got used to seeing
them, like Mr. Geyer said. Even so, people glance at someone when they enter a room or walk down a sidewalk, out
of simple curiosity.

And Margaret! She could have been killed when she
stepped into the street. Yet she did not appear the least bit
troubled. She was sitting across from me, in front of Mr.
Geyer. Her eyes were closed against the sunlight as she
rested her head on the back of the seat.

Mr. Geyer had stared out the window most of the way
home looking pale and drained. At one point, I had leaned
over and touched him on the shoulder, to make sure he

was okay. He had given me a weary smile and shook his head as if he couldn't imagine what he would have done if he had lost her. Yet the strangest part of the day occurred when we got to our stop. I thought about Margaret and the big smile she had given to the jitney driver as we exited. The driver was an old guy with thick eyebrows and a hunched back. He winked at her as she called good-bye. Why was he able to see her, when people in town had not?

I kept replaying yesterday in my mind as I sat at the kitchen table, staring vacantly at my cemetery poster propped in the kitchen bay window. It was almost noontime. Dad was at work. Mom was running a bunch of errands. We were all supposed to be practicing for the event tomorrow, but I was having trouble concentrating. I was anxious about the cemetery tour. I was nervous about yesterday. Come to think of it, I had been consistently edgy ever since I met Margaret and Mr. Geyer. Not because of them, of course, but because of the things that had been happening to me since I had met them. Yet at the same time, I felt alive. I never remembered my life being so full of adventure. I sipped at my glass of ice water and hoped the cold sliding down my throat would jolt me into action.

Margaret and Mr. Geyer were prepping at their house, and were to come over tonight so that we could practice our routine in front of Mom and Dad. Mr. Geyer had sketched out tomorrow's event. Margaret and I were to stand by our posters after Mr. Geyer completed his brief cemetery tour, ready to explain the history and meaning behind the photos we chose. I looked at my poster. It seemed out of place against the pastel blue sky, although the ivy hanging outside the window made an appropriate frame for it. I had to make sure that I knew each photograph as if the people remembered were my own family. Only then, Mr. Geyer had said, would I be able to stir something in other people's hearts. I did not dare let Margaret and Mr. Geyer down.

I studied the black-and-white photos. I had carefully captioned each in large black letters so that someone in the back of the crowd could read them. Margaret had said the lettering looked Gothic and then did the same with her poster.

The photo in the top left corner was the grave of the Fletcher children. At first, all one saw was the huge slab of stone, shaped like the A frame of a house. But once you peered at it, you could not help but recoil from the sneering skeleton head on top, his wings huddled possessively around the carved names beneath them. Each name was crowned with its own small symbol. John, six years, had the crossbones, while Sarah, three years, had an hourglass. Ann, nine weeks, had an angel, not as angry looking as most I had seen in the cemetery.

The next photo was of a little boy's tombstone. Mr. Geyer had told me about the stonecutter who had carved this stone. He had been an acquaintance of Christian's. In most of the stones this man carved, the Death head symbol was always wide-eyed and calm, looking fairly untroubled to people passing by the grave site. Mr. Geyer said that the art on this tombstone gave a person the sense that death was not something to dread—until it came for this stone-cutter's own son. Little Joshua's Death head had an angry expression, its eyes near slits, its forehead shortened, and its teeth scrupulously cut. I remembered Mr. Geyer telling me that Christian never carved another stone after Prudence's death, although Joshua's father apparently did nothing else but crank out angry angel after angry angel. Each man handled his burdens quite differently, he noted without irony.

I stared at the other tombstones captured in our photographs, amazed that I felt a real sorrow for them, even though the people they remembered had been gone from this world for more than two hundred years. There was

Ebenezer, the shipwrecked sailor. Patience, the young mother of four and the reverend's wife. The most heartbreaking of all was the baby's stone. The name had been maliciously scratched out because the infant had been born out of wedlock.

Skeletons, angels, urns, fountains, Death heads, suns, and moons, and everything with wings—they were all mesmerizing, but not scary. It made me sad to think of the long-lost lives, yet happy that their memories had been so preciously preserved. When I had told this to Mr. Geyer, he smiled and said that that was precisely what I should say to people. I must make them feel a kinship, he said, as if those people remembered by stones could be our own family and friends.

I must have been practicing for at least an hour. My throat felt scratchy from talking out loud like Mr. Geyer had instructed, but I was feeling a little more confident because I could now just look at one of the photos and talk about it without memorizing a word-for-word summary. I was ready for our practice run tonight as I went to the window to move the poster to a safe place. I inhaled in surprise when I saw them.

Cats. A small mob of them in the backyard, milling around on the lawn between the patio and the shed. I tried counting the tabbies, oranges, calicos, and the one black cat. They were circling one another with their tails in the air and meowing as if they were having a meeting. I tallied ten in all. What were they doing here? I had never seen cats in our yard. Were they the feral cats that Margaret and Mr. Geyer fed?

I slipped out the back door to stand on our patio to stare at them. I felt the laser-like heat of the sun on the back of my neck, tasted the dry tinge of pine in the air, smelled the sweetness of the dry grass, and heard the calls of the blackbirds that gathered in the woods. I watched the cats suddenly stop their circling to raise their heads simultaneously, as if they were listening to something. As a group, they began to walk, slowly at first with that confident, measured gait that only cats seem capable of, to the border of the woods along the back of our yard. They continued until they reached the thick growth of pine trees and then disappeared.

I squinted at their point of entry and could make out what looked like a row of small rocks. I had not noticed the rocks there two days ago when I did the weeding. *Go over and look at them,* I chanted before I left the safety of the patio. All the while I listened for the sound the cats had heard coming from the woods. All I could hear was the birds.

The rocks glinted in the sun as I approached, despite the snarl of weeds that partially covered them. I kicked at one of them cautiously. They were not rocks but opened cat food tins, just like the ones that were lined up along Margaret and Mr. Geyer's house. Mom and Dad would never have put these here. They hardly had the time to hang around out back. Would Margaret or Mr. Geyer be leaving cat food all over the edge of the woods? My heart revved up a notch.

I peered nervously into the labyrinth of trees. There were no paths that led to our yard, at least there were no *clear* paths. When I focused really hard, I could just barely make out the remnants of a path pitching toward the center of the woods, where the branches of the pine trees and scrub interlaced. I squinted into the forest shade. It was early afternoon and the sun was blazing. Yet the thickness of the woods muffled the light. I took a few tentative steps and listened to the scratching of the cicadas and the call of some lonely bird.

And then I saw her—her face—pale as the moon in a black sky. She was kneeling by a cluster of trees two hundred yards away. I held my breath as I watched her dig. Her shoulders trembled as she cut at the earth. I was rooted to the spot. She stood and placed something in the pocket of her cloak, then turned and headed deeper into the woods.

My heart was pounding so ferociously that all I could

hear now was my own pulse. Could I follow her without her knowing it? Didn't witches have extra-keen senses?

I crouched automatically as I began to work my way through the tangle of branches and vines, trying hard not to snap twigs or rustle dead leaves. *Walk like an Indian,* I kept telling myself, although I did not have a clue as to how Indians learned to be so silent on their feet.

I had gone too far to turn back. My eyes stung from my sweat and I had a random thought about ticks in the woods, but within moments I froze. There was the witch in a small clearing surrounding a cluster of trees less than a hundred yards away. I held my breath.

The witch was laying something on the ground beneath a tree whose trunk must have been three feet in diameter. Its roots bulged from the ground like giant worms, and its branches thrust in all directions like thick, gnarled arms. The tree must have stood at least one hundred feet high.

I watched the witch pull something from her pocket and sprinkle it onto the earth. She began to hum and then to chant in a singsong voice. She raised her arms to the sky, like she was begging or demanding something. In a moment, her arms dropped back to her sides. She turned and disappeared deeper into the woods.

I must have stood in that spot for at least a half hour. I dared not move to the tree until I was sure that the witch

would not return. Finally I thought I was safe and took a few silent steps to the spot where the witch had been reciting a spell.

The earth beneath the canopy of the tree was bare. Fresh ivy formed a border in the shape of a cemetery plot. Was that all I could think about? Then I noticed the bark of the tree. Ivy shapes—just like those in my basement—carved into the trunk of the tree from its roots to about six feet high.

I gasped and reached out to touch it. Then I felt something stringy and cold around my ankle. I looked down to see a vine of ivy wrapping around my shin.

I screamed and jumped to brush it off, but suddenly the once-bare ground was a bed of slithering, convulsing ivy. Vines were creeping like snakes to tangle themselves around my feet and legs.

I screamed again. I no longer cared about the witch. The ivy was trying to strangle me! I tore it away from my legs, stamping at it as it withered on the ground beneath my feet. Surprisingly, it didn't have the same death grip it had when Dad had tried to pull it from the walls of our house. This ivy seemed to let go when I yanked at it, like its efforts were only halfhearted. When I was finally free of the vines, I plunged toward the rough path in the woods that I had made. All I wanted to do was get home.

"Courtney," someone whispered. I stopped as if I had no choice. I turned to see the witch standing by the tree now. Her black cloak was wrapped around her, and her green eyes were incandescent in the darkness of the woods. Her smile was pleased. The ivy was looping around her boots.

She raised her hand to beckon me to her.

"No!" I yelled at her as I pitched myself back down my path toward home.

I stood on our patio to catch my breath before I went into the house. I could not go inside like this—shaking as if I were freezing. Yet the sweat running down my face told me that I was not cold.

I stared at the cat food tins, which I had scattered all over the yard as I tumbled out of the woods. Not a graceful exit. I almost expected the cats to reappear on cue, the way cats seem to come out of nowhere when someone turns on a can opener, but they did not return. I smoothed my tangled hair with my hands and was still breathing like I had just run a marathon. For a moment, I thought I heard the whinny of a horse far off in the woods, but I was unsure.

I looked at my legs and the scratches on my ankles and shins, proof of my terrifying race through the woods and not the ivy clawing at me, because my arms were scratched, too. *Those ivy vines—were they really wrapping themselves around my legs and feet or was that just my imagination?* I had not noticed the ivy in the clearing when I had first reached it. Then suddenly it was there, all over the ground, writhing as if it were being boiled. The ivy . . . the same ivy clung to the walls of our house. I whipped around to see it fluttering innocently in the breeze.

A sudden noise in the kitchen nearly made me scream, but I caught a glimpse of Mom through the bay window, leaning over the sink, doing the dishes. She was home! I weakened with relief.

I could not tell Mom what happened. I was worried that after I told them about witches and crazed ivy, she and Dad would never let me help Mr. Geyer and Margaret with their campaign to save the cemetery. She would be sure that my imagination was getting out of control because of the stories I heard about the people buried in the cemetery. Even though she did not know about Christian's journal and his spooky connection to the ivy, Mom would decide that this cemetery project was not really healthy for a girl my age if it made me hallucinate. I could not let that happen. I would tell Margaret and Mr. Geyer about the witch and the cats. They at least would have some theories.

"Courtney! What on earth happened to you?!" Mom cried. She froze in mid-reach for a hand towel.

My heart thumped against my rib cage.

"Hi, Mom," I replied, as if out of breath from exercise. I wondered if I sounded too perky. "I saw a bunch of cats in the yard and chased them into the woods. I was curious about where they had come from," I added lamely.

"Jeez, Courtney. Look how scratched up you are." She came at me with a washcloth that she had just held under the faucet. "Sit down," she instructed as she gently cleaned the scratches on my arm. "You need to be more careful. Does it hurt?" Her nose was scrunched up in the way it does when she thinks something is wrong. "Are you sure nothing else happened?"

"Mom, I'm fine," I insisted, figuring that I was telling the truth indirectly. She crouched beside me and stared into my eyes, her own blue eyes sharp and probing.

"Okay, but I want you to put some antiseptic on those scratches when you go upstairs." She paused for a moment, giving my legs a last swipe. "Are you anxious about tomorrow?" she asked. "I know I am." Her words were eager and clipped, the way she spoke about a topic that excited her.

"Mom, sit down. *You're* making me anxious!" I said. "But I guess I am a little nervous. I don't want to mess up.

I practiced all morning for the cemetery event." I glanced in the direction of the cemetery, as if I could see it through the kitchen wall. Mom slipped into the chair beside me. "I think I know every bat, hourglass, and Death head on my poster by heart."

She crossed her legs and began to jiggle her foot. And she accused *me* of being jittery. "You're going to do fine, Courtney. I hope Mr. Geyer knows how lucky he is to have you on his side." She cupped her chin in her hand as she rested her elbow on the table, silent for a moment.

"Was your article published today?" I asked. Bizarrely, I wondered if the witch might read the paper.

"I'm glad you reminded me!" she exclaimed as she shot out of her chair. "It's on the counter." She glanced out the window as she picked up her folder. "I think we'll have a good crowd, Courtney, if the weather holds up. I heard on the radio that there's a slight chance of thunderstorms."

She slid back into her chair as I opened *The Murmur Mercury.*

"Hey, Mom, the article looks great," I said. There was a big photo of the cemetery entrance with the *Memento Mori* sign. The article was titled the same.

"Do you think so?" she asked warmly. "I tried to cover so much—the history of the cemetery and the important families buried there. I ended the article with our current crisis, noting how sprawl was decimating our country's pre-cious green spaces." Her lips were pursed as she stared at the print. "I hope it's not overwhelming. People today don't seem to have the greatest attention span."

I looked at her and smiled. It always amazed me that she was able to collect and summarize so much informa-tion so quickly. Is that what passion does for you? Does it give you the edge you need when you are fighting for something? Then Mr. Geyer and Margaret should surely be able to find Prudence. "I think it sounds great, and I know Mr. Geyer will be thrilled," I assured her.

She touched me affectionately on the cheek. "Come on. Go put some antiseptic on those cuts and then come grocery shopping with me. We'll have burgers tonight since the Geyers are coming over for rehearsal."

I nodded. Seven o'clock could not come fast enough for me.

THE MURMUR MERCURY

AUGUST 21, 2008

Memento Mori:
Historic Murmur Cemetery
Threatened by Development

by Jennifer O'Brien

When this writer recently moved to Murmur, Mass., urban sprawl was the furthest thing from her mind. However, the historic nineteenth century Memento Mori Cemetery has caught the eye of developer Morris McGarrity, CEO and founder of Greener Pastures, Inc., a real estate and development firm based in New York City. According to McGarrity, the demand for new luxury homes in our region is high, and Murmur's vast farmlands are productive, with owners having connections to their land going back centuries. Mr. McGarrity approached the Murmur Town Council regarding his potential interest in purchasing one hundred acres of cemetery parcels instead. New homes will mean a growing tax base for a town like Murmur that forecasts a new elementary and high school in the not-too-distant future.

chapter 9

M R. GEYER AND MARGARET STOOD ON OUR FRONT
steps at five minutes past seven. The leaves of
the massive oak tree in our front yard quivered
in the slight evening breeze.

"Hey, should be a nice day tomorrow," I announced,
bursting to tell them about the witch.

Margaret cocked her head and smiled. "It had better
be," she agreed.

Mr. Geyer stood quietly in his black shorts and red
checkered shirt, his backpack slung over his shoulder. He
gave me an amused smile. Margaret looked radiant—her
green eyes sparkling against her blushed cheeks. Her hair
was in a loose ponytail again. She must be feeling confident
about tomorrow, which made my own spirits rise. Her
poster was safely tucked under her arm.

Mom breezed into the foyer and shook Mr. Geyer's
hand while beaming a mischievous smile at Margaret. "Did

you see the article in today's paper?" Her chin was raised expectantly.

Mr. Geyer smiled and nodded. "Yes, I did. It was very well done. I'm confident that it will deliver the crowd we're hoping for."

Mom smiled in appreciation, still pumping his hand. "I'm glad you liked it." She glanced at me, telling me with her eyes that everything was going to be all right. "Let's go into the kitchen. There's plenty of room for us to practice for tomorrow, and Tom has started a pot of coffee." As she said it, the aroma of coffee wafted into the hall.

Dad suddenly materialized beneath the kitchen and dining room arch. He crossed the dining room, scooting expertly around the table, to shake Mr. Geyer's hand.

"Christian, how are you?" Dad's voice was warm and sincere. Mom must have given him a pep talk.

"I'll be able to give you a better response tomorrow afternoon, when our event is behind us," Mr. Geyer replied, releasing Dad's hand to adjust his glasses. I knew Mr. Geyer well enough by now to recognize his nervous quirks, but his voice was steady. "Courtney and Jennifer have been extremely supportive. Margaret and I are very lucky to have met such good people."

Dad glanced at me and smiled. "Well, I'm a little late coming into the game. So I want you to use me tonight as your objective audience. At least I'll be able to tell you what themes tug at my heart."

"Splendid idea," Mr. Geyer agreed.

Mom, the organizer, interrupted to get us back on track. "Why don't we, the audience, sit around the kitchen table facing the windows. There's plenty of space for you to stand and move about. We'll use our imagination to pretend that you're standing at the cemetery entrance. Margaret, you can prop your poster next to Courtney's on the shelf of the bay window."

I moved my poster over as Margaret leaned hers against the window. She stared for a second past the ivy that brushed loosely against the windowpane and then looked at me. The yard was empty and quiet in the twilight. Did she know that I was checking for witches or cats?

We were an attentive audience for Mr. Geyer. We all sat politely, mindful not to squirm in our seats or sneak peeks at the posters. Soon I was hypnotized by his stories. He projected his voice as if he were addressing a crowd, and waved his arms and gestured as if he were on a stage. Mr. Geyer planned to dress as a Puritan tomorrow and shared with us the story he would tell of the burial of a wealthy merchant to illustrate the Puritans' belief that funerals should be celebrations.

He spoke of Elijah Watson, who died in his seventh

decade, leaving his third wife, eight children, and five grand-children behind. Mr. Watson was a contemporary of Cotton Mather, the famous Puritan minister and writer who supported the Salem witch trials. News of Mr. Watson's death would have spread quickly through the town, he said, and the town's craftsmen and stonecutters would have received the orders to produce Mr. Watson's hatchments for the funeral display—diamond-shaped panels bearing his coat of arms, glue-stiffened cloths with Mr. Watson's shield, and smaller crests to decorate his home. Mr. Geyer pulled a few samples of these decorations from his backpack with the air of mystery magicians use when they are pulling surprises out of a hat.

"And contrary to popular belief, the Puritans were capable of a little celebration, particularly when it involved sending a fellow citizen into the hereafter," he continued with enthusiasm. "Even the horses would be decorated with these symbols as a solemn procession followed the carriage to the burial grounds. After the prayers were said, there would be a feast probably unlike any Mr. Watson enjoyed while he was alive, unless he happened to have been invited to another man's funeral. For Puritans lived in the presence of the Black Angel," Mr. Geyer explained dramatically, "and came to not fear him."

"Is that a true story?" my dad finally asked, breaking

the silence. He was holding my mother's hand.

"Of course." Mr. Geyer smiled. "And while I still have you perched on the edge of your chairs, let me give you an overview of tomorrow's tour," he teased, pulling a map of the cemetery out of his bag. He pointed out the various grave sites and tombstones that would be visited. I noticed that he didn't stray anywhere near Prudence's grave.

"Then I will direct the *crowd*, and I use the word hopefully," he interjected, "to stop to see the girls and their posters by the entrance and to ask them about their research."

"That's our cue," Margaret said as she nudged me. We dutifully stood up and marched to our posters. Margaret volunteered to explain hers first as Dad and Mom stood beside us, peering intently at the photographs. They made interested or sympathetic noises as we explained the circumstances of each picture. By the end, Mom had tears in her eyes.

"I'm so proud of you both," she sniffed. Mom had always been an emotional person.

Dad put his arm around her shoulder. "Great work, girls. You'd have to be dead not to be touched by this." Margaret and I rolled our eyes at his intentional pun. "Anyway, how about some coffee, soda, and dessert? You deserve a reward for all of this hard work."

Margaret turned to me and said, "Courtney said she wanted to show me something in her bedroom first. Can you all excuse us for a few minutes?"

I looked at Margaret, amazed. *How did she know I needed to talk to her?*

"Certainly. We'll be sure to save you some goodies." My dad was already pouring the coffee and pulling out a chair for Mr. Geyer.

We made it only as far as the hallway when Margaret grabbed my wrist. "What is it, Courtney?" she whispered. "You looked like you were ready to burst as soon as I saw you." Her green eyes were wide, her gaze penetrating. I looked at the hallway closet and beside it at the closed basement door, shadowed now as the sun had set.

I shivered, suddenly cold as I recalled this afternoon's events. I told her everything—about the cats in our backyard, the witch doing weird things in the woods, the tree with the ivy carved into its bark, and the ivy wrapping itself around my ankles, holding me to the spot. It was like a scary fairy tale—cats luring the unsuspecting girl into the witch's woods.

Her grip loosened and I rubbed my wrist without thinking. Margaret wrinkled her nose, perplexed. She glanced over her shoulder in the direction of the laughter coming from the kitchen.

"I don't think the ivy would harm you, Courtney. Perhaps the witch was using it to tell you something." Her voice was suddenly breathless. "She uses the cats that way. That's why we feed them. Of course we feed them because they're hungry, too, and it's the humane thing to do," she added quickly. "But we can tell when the witch is around, because the cats act nervous and stay together. They're always listening to something that we can't hear, as you saw happen in your yard today."

"I don't know, Margaret. That ivy scared me," I insisted. If the witch was trying to tell me something, she had a strange way of getting my attention. "And besides, what would she possibly want to tell *me*?" This was the thing that unnerved me the most. I never had believed in wicked witches, invisible ghosts, or haunted ivy.

"I bet you believe now," Margaret retorted.

Before I had the chance to ask her how she kept reading my mind, she put her finger to her lips to shush me. "We need to check the ivy in the basement," she said softly, probably afraid that she was going to give me a heart attack. I knew that she was going to suggest this, even though *I* couldn't read minds.

I nodded. "I couldn't go down there without you," I said.

She peeked around the corner and seemed satisfied that

our parents were still at the table. Then she grabbed my hand and opened the basement door.

I clicked on the light as we tiptoed down the stairs. All of the boards creaked but the laughter and conversation coming from the kitchen smothered our sounds. From the bottom of the steps, the basement appeared as it did the last time. The sickly yellow light cast from the lonely bulbs barely illuminated the stored furniture and the boxes lined up along the far wall.

I thought Margaret was going to crush the bones in my hand as we approached the carved ivy. Dad and Mom had moved the boxes away from the wall enough to give them a better look the last time they were down here. We were only halfway across the basement floor when I saw that the ivy had blossomed from its original patch to spread to the entire wall and part of the ceiling.

"Courtney, when did this happen?" Margaret gazed at the ceiling, her mouth open.

"I don't know," I replied weakly. My knees felt wobbly. "Why does it look so angry?" I asked. The original carvings had been faint and curved softly as the vines seemed to twine along the wall. I could not find a better way to describe the sharp twists and turns its vines seemed to dig into the stone as if it had gone berserk.

"Courtney, stop," Margaret warned in a high, unnatural

voice. The sound of it made my hair stand on end. I turned to her. Her face was white. She stared at the floor now.

There, between the ivy-covered wall and the boxes that we had pushed into the center of the basement, ivy was being chiseled by invisible hands into the slate of the floor. The sudden, staccato sound of a hammer on metal reminded me of little firecrackers—snappy and defiant. Before our eyes, the ivy formed a straight line and then took a turn at a right angle. Its work was done within seconds.

I wanted to scream but nothing came out. For the second time today, my heart attempted to bash its way out of my chest. I grabbed Margaret's hand and yanked her toward the basement stairway. All I could think about was the ivy coming alive and wrapping itself around my ankles, angrier now, as it had failed once already today.

But Margaret resisted my tugging. "Courtney, wait," she pleaded. I could barely hear her above the pounding in my head. She turned her face toward me. It looked drained of all color but she shook her head, trying to slow me down.

"It's the witch," she insisted. "She's trying to tell us something. We must listen." She let go of my hand, allowing me to dash up the stairs. She was obviously staying right there.

I stood my ground. I could not leave Margaret. I tried my best to slow my heart as Margaret stared at the newly carved ivy. "It's forming the outline of a cemetery plot, I think," she said in wonder. Her hands were now cupped over her mouth. As soon as she said it, I knew she was right, for the chiseled ivy took the exact same shape as the ivy plot that the witch had made beneath the tree in the woods. A map for gravediggers.

"Is this a good thing?" I croaked. Margaret would know, I told myself. Margaret had studied signs from the witch her whole life, but she said nothing. In less than a minute, someone—or something—had finished their work. A carved border of ivy in the shape of a coffin was inscribed forever into the basement floor.

Margaret nodded, never turning from the ivy. "Dad believes that any attempt to communicate is a good thing." Despite her calm, I could feel her trembling. Or was that me?

Suddenly, more than anything in the world, I wanted to tell my parents everything.

"Is the witch on our side?" I asked her, this time leading her more gently toward the basement door. I did not want to take any chances in case the witch decided to give the ivy life.

"Dad thinks so," she replied. Her eyes were watery as she looked back at the floor. "I think so," she added more softly. "But I can't be sure. Read this," she said fiercely as she pulled a folded paper from her pocket.

I opened the paper, amazed that Margaret and I were having this conversation just yards away from new ivy carvings. It was another excerpt from Christian's journal.

Margaret looked at the ceiling, at the spot where Mr. Geyer might be sitting. "I didn't tell Dad that I copied this page, because I didn't want to worry him."

"Why couldn't you tell your dad?" I asked. This was unlike Margaret.

"Because I needed to know something. Something that I couldn't ask Dad about."

Margaret was looking down again at the ivy. This time there was no ambivalence in her face. I wanted to ask Margaret how she could be afraid to tell Mr. Geyer something, and yet have no fear of this ivy blazing its own paths across my basement floor. But I could not ask here, in the presence of the miraculously growing ivy.

"Go ahead. Read it now, before we go upstairs, but don't read it out loud," she whispered.

The paper contained Margaret's deliberate script. I took a deep breath and began to read.

Wherever I go, there is ivy. The ivy and I are one now, it seems.

The witch said that it is in my blood, as it is in her blood, and this is how it must be for the ivy to do its work.

"Is that why the ivy breeds where I go, on whatever I touch?" I asked her.

She smiled at me like a pupil.

"Yes. It will bring us together, all of us together. It will bind us until we are one. The ivy is our talisman."

I turned from her. I was unsure if I understood the ivy's power.

She cocked her head at my reluctance and took my hand in her cold one.

"The cemetery and this house—they are your heart, your spirit. And the spirits that come after you will fade, will shimmer into dust, should they leave this site. For here is your Prudence."

"Margaret," I looked up from the paper. A sudden realization hit me in the stomach.

"Don't say it," she commanded, placing her fingers over my lips. "We must go upstairs now." She took the paper and put it back into her pocket. The banister squealed under the weight of her hand.

"I should tell my parents about this," I said, more calmly than I would have thought possible minutes ago.

"No, Courtney," she said, turning to face me. "The witch is active. I've never seen her so active. If you tell your parents, everything could be ruined." Her eyes were pleading.

I paused, my heart still doing somersaults. Margaret seemed so sure that the witch and her ivy—real or carved—were helping us to solve the mystery of Prudence.

"Margaret, how do you know that the witch is good?" I pleaded.

She put her hand over her mouth and shook her head before she answered me. "I can't tell you yet, Courtney. But I know. Will you trust me? We need your help."

I knew then that I would not tell my parents, not tonight anyway. Margaret was right. Once they saw the ivy for themselves, they would know something bizarre was going on and they would take me away from here until they could explain it.

I reached for her hand. "I trust you, Margaret. And I want to help you and your dad. I promised I would," I added.

She took a deep breath and smiled. "You'll see, Courtney. Soon you'll understand." But just before she opened the basement door, she turned to me, her green eyes fierce. "I *am* going to tell Dad about this," she said, as if recognizing my need to have some adult informed about today's events. "And if he thinks there is any danger, we will be back tonight."

THE MURMUR MERCURY

Weather Watch   AUGUST 22, 2008

Blue skies and sun are in today's forecast, with a light breeze and temperatures touching the high eighties. Beautiful day for picnicking, biking, playing ball, or strolling along Murmur's Main Street to take advantage of the annual Sidewalk Sale. We've all heard the cliché about "not a cloud in sight." Today is truly one of those cloudless days.

—Weather Watch, sponsored by the Murmur Chamber of Commerce

chapter 10

I SHOULD HAVE BEEN BLEARY-EYED, BUT INSTEAD I HAD THE
worst case of butterflies, just like I do when I have to
take an oral test or perform in a school play. It was only
nine o'clock as I stood before the cemetery entrance with
my poster at my side. We were supposed to meet at ten to
prepare, but I needed to be out in the warm air and sun-
shine. My insides had felt cold all night. Besides, here it was
quiet. Only the birds and squirrels could be heard, with the
exception of the occasional car as it whooshed by on the
open road. There was no breeze, and the cornstalks across
the street seemed to be stretching to touch the sky. This was
much better than listening to Mom and Dad chattering
away over breakfast, giving me public speaking tips, and
reminding me to smile. I was not in the mood for a parental
pep talk.

Last night I could not sleep for even a minute. I listened
all night for the sound of chiseling—of those invisible hands

carving the ivy into something that was now bare—the floorboards, the banisters, and the doors. Of course, I never heard it.

Although I must have carved my own path in my bedroom rug as I paced from my bed to the window to stare into the yard and the cemetery darkness. I squinted at the white ghostly forms—the tombstones—as if I expected them to suddenly uproot and run. I was also looking for the cats, the witch, or the ivy, all of which could suddenly be on the move.

And I thought about Margaret, about the page from Christian's journal, and the witch's vow that Christian's descendants' spirits "will fade and shimmer into dust should they leave this site." Is that why the people in Murmur did not see Mr. Geyer and Margaret? Their souls or spirits were too far from the ivy and the place of Christian's and Prudence's burial grounds when they were in town. Did that mean that Christian and Prudence must be buried somewhere around here? I needed to ask Margaret about this.

I propped my poster against the stone column and wrapped my hands around the iron bars of the gate. The metal still held the chill of the evening. I glanced toward Prudence's gravestone—all seemed okay. In the gentle morning light, the tilted tombstones appeared almost

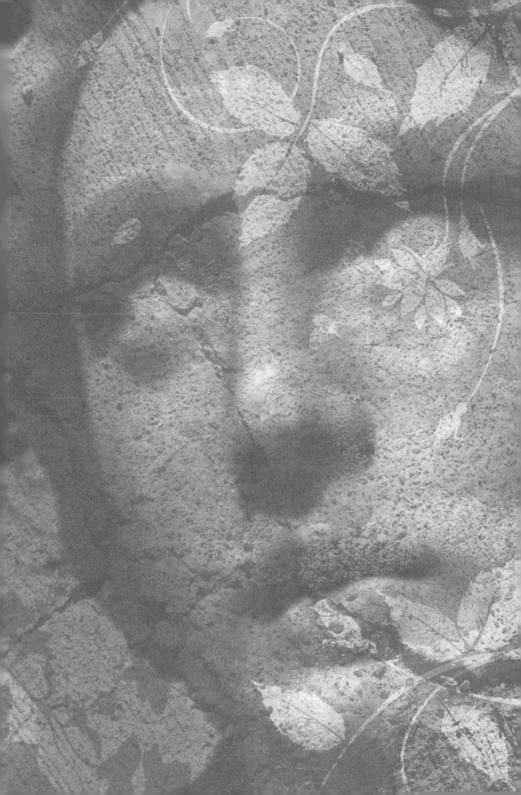

giddy compared to last night, as if they were all just a little bit tipsy. The leaves of the willow and sycamore trees, which formed the borders of the many paths, seemed to droop in sleep. Such a quiet, peaceful site. Why did darkness make me feel so afraid, when all it did was hide such tranquility?

I heard voices soft with the sound of laughter. I looked down the road toward my house to see Margaret carrying her poster in front of her. She walked beside a Pilgrim or, I guess, a Puritan, with a sack flung over his shoulder. Mr. Geyer was wearing one of those cone-shaped hats with a wide brim and a buckle in the center. His black shoes had buckles, too. All his clothes were black except for his white shirt with the poofy collar that seemed to hang limply over his black coat. The best part was seeing Mr. Geyer in knickers and stockings. Margaret pointed at them as she walked beside him, and he reached over to playfully pull at her ponytail. He really did look like a guy who had just walked out of the eithteenth century.

"Hello, Courtney. Are you ready for our big show?" Margaret's face was flushed, her eyes bright. The pinched look of worry she carried from our house last night was gone. Mr. Geyer gently lowered his sack onto the driveway.

"Well, what do you think?" he asked, raising his arms, as if begging for an answer. "Do I look the part?"

I looked at his lens-enhanced eyes beneath his big hat. "You look great," I replied sincerely. "Are Pilgrims and Puritans the same thing? You look like a Pilgrim going to a funeral."

Mr. Geyer laughed. "Well, they both were fleeing religious persecution and did dress similarly. The Puritans were a bit grim, though. Thus the choice of black." He looked down at his buckles proudly.

"He stood in front of the mirror for about an hour this morning," Margaret teased, rolling her eyes.

A passing car slowed to gawk at Mr. Geyer. He waved good-naturedly.

"Aren't you going to be hot?" I asked, feeling the threads of my shirt warming as the sun's hands were on my back.

"Yes, but I won't mind it, Courtney, because passion makes it easier to bear many discomforts," he said seriously.

"He even *sounds* like a Puritan," Margaret said.

"I'm in character, my dear girl," he replied with the barest of smiles. "We have only one shot today to convince the good residents of Murmur that they must save their Puritan cemetery."

"Are you ready, Courtney?" Margaret asked, clinging to her poster. Her knuckles were white.

"Sure I am," I said with too much gusto. I needed Margaret to be the confident one. "Mom and Dad have the easels. Dad borrowed them from work. They'll be here soon to help us set up." Suddenly I felt all business.

"Splendid," Mr. Geyer replied. "Why don't you girls go over your posters one last time while I review my notes? We want this to be perfect."

I glanced into the cemetery, toward Prudence's grave. *I hope you appreciate all the work they are doing.* The Geyers were determined to break whatever nasty spell the witch had placed on all of them.

By the time a second wave of cars pulled up to the cemetery gate, there were already about fifteen people standing in the driveway apron, waiting for the tour. Mr. Geyer directed people to park their cars on the side of the narrow gravel road, which split the cemetery in half like a drunken line. Margaret and I giggled at the Puritan parking lot attendant. The single road was the only one available to cars, and funeral participants were forced to walk quite a distance along the narrow pathways to get to graveside services that were on the fringes of the cemetery. Mr. Geyer said that the gravel road was actually the original road for the horse-drawn funeral hearses. I shook my head.

I knew way too much about this cemetery.

Mom smiled brightly at the visitors around our posters as she clutched her notepad and pen. A camera was slung over her shoulder. I watched her approach a young couple, extending her hand, causing them to release each other's. She pointed to her notebook, her eyebrows raised expectantly. The couple nodded as she wrote down their names.

Dad was busy reviewing the schedule, as he called it, with Mr. Geyer. He was rubbing his chin and pointing in various directions as he mulled over the itinerary. Mr. Geyer had a patient, amused smile on his face, although I could see he was a little nervous because he kept adjusting his glasses. Margaret and I stood by one of the easels that Dad had placed by both entrance columns.

The late-morning sun was blinding, and I raised my hand over my eyes to squint at our crowd. The people who had arrived early were older—bald men wearing cheap sneakers and big shorts, ladies with white hair, sensible shoes, and skirts, clutching their purses to their chests. They seemed nice, though. Lots of squinty smiles softened lined faces. Obviously people who liked this sort of thing and had the time to arrive early to hang for a while. Two of the people had dragged kids along—kids old enough to walk without complaining too much. I figured they had babysitting duty for the grandchildren.

The rest of the crowd contained people of all ages, who clustered in family or friends' groups as they stood in the driveway on both sides of the cemetery gate. I even recognized a few faces—the tall, thin librarian from town, the nervous manager from the grocery store, the cute guy with the mustache who coached the peewee soccer team. Passing the soccer field on our way into town was one of the highlights of our drives. Both Mom and I loved to see the little kids tumbling over the ball like bowling pins. Even the kid from the pizza shop was there, this time wearing a black Alice Cooper T-shirt. I felt myself turn red when he waved at me.

"Good morning, guests!" Mr. Geyer bellowed from the cemetery entrance. "*Memento Mori!*" he added with gusto, looking up at the ironwork that proclaimed just the same directly over his head.

Mr. Geyer raised his arms and motioned for everyone to gather around him. He smiled as if he was among friends. "Of course, you all are just the type of people that the Puritans would appreciate," he said jokingly, "as you are 'remembering death' by your supportive presence here today." There was some polite laughter as people glanced at one another shyly. And then he was off. Mr. Geyer seemed born to teach and reenact history. I felt the tension in my muscles draining away as he told the crowd about the history of the cemetery, the interest in preserving it, and the important role this cemetery played in the history of Murmur. "Your founding fathers are here," he extolled. "Those brave settlers, who left Europe to carve out a new way of life. Their bones are in these fields." He turned to gaze at the crop of tombstones behind him. When he faced the crowd again, I thought I saw the glimmer of tears in his eyes. "The men who fought in our war for independence are laid here, as are the men who fought to keep our country together. And the mothers, wives, and daughters who embraced this challenging way of life, who nurtured Murmur till it grew to be the wonderful town it is today, they are here beneath this grassy blanket."

I glanced over at Mom and Dad. They both looked around at the crowd as if gauging people's reactions. Margaret's gaze was glued to Mr. Geyer. She stood as straight as a soldier. I looked out over the many faces. Some were nodding and smiling. Others were trying to peer over Mr. Geyer's shoulders as if they couldn't wait to get into the cemetery. They all looked interested. Had any of them been on one of Mr. Geyer's previous tours?

Mr. Geyer bent down and pulled out a few of the hatchments—the shields with a family's coat of arms—that he shared with us last night. The crowd moved in a few steps closer, until Mr. Geyer began passing them around among the group. He launched into his story about the funeral of Elijah Watson, whose death provided a grand diversion for the otherwise monotonous lives of Murmur's populace. A great funeral was an event to look forward to, as the money saved by the frugal Puritans was often spent to provide a heavenly send-off for the deceased that was unparalleled to any festivity sponsored when the now departed was alive.

Mr. Geyer's stories about Cotton Mather involved the Puritan preacher's role in the late seventeenth century witch trials. Preacher Mather supported the use of "spectral evidence" as testimony that the accused witch's spirit had appeared to the witness in a dream or vision. The dream or vision was admitted as evidence. Witnesses, who were often also the accusers, would testify that the "witch" had bitten, pinched, and pushed them to the ground. The dream was taken as evidence that the accused were responsible for the biting, pinching, and pushing, even though they were elsewhere at the time.

A tittering thrill seemed to sweep the crowd. Mom had told me the night before that it was important to add some sensational elements to a story to keep people's interest. Mom snapped a picture from the side.

It was not until we went into the cemetery, to see some of the tombstones that Mr. Geyer had chosen to illustrate the artwork of the stonecutters, that the sun was suddenly smothered by some rumbling dark clouds.

———

"Come, friends. Follow me to the resting place of Beatrice Wolcott, where we will begin our discussion of the grave-stone art." Mr. Geyer raised his arm and gestured to the crowd to follow him. They were right on his heels, as some moms grabbed kids' hands or old guys in white shorts gently touched the white-haired ladies' elbows. I heard the click of Mom's camera. "If you need to leave the tour early, be sure to stop and view the posters designed by Courtney and Margaret. They show a few more sites that aren't included in my walking tour." Some people looked back and gave us an encouraging smile, as if they wouldn't *think* of missing us.

Mom and Dad were at the tail end of the group. Mom was looking up at the sky, her brows furrowed quizzically. Had she heard a rumbling? I anxiously searched the sky and spotted some dark clouds in the distance. *Stay there,* I commanded.

After a few minutes, Margaret and I left our posts to stand on the other side of the columned entrance. We wanted to watch Mr. Geyer's progress. From this distance, although he was really never far, we saw him wave his arms dramatically or drop down to peer at a stone. He even took off his hat in a sweeping motion, indicating to the crowd the direction to flow to reach the next gravesite. Mom and Dad whispered to each other from the fringe, nodding sometimes. I was relieved that people looked interested. Many of them tilted their heads as Mr. Geyer spoke or raised their hands when he took a breather.

"Such an actor," Margaret commented dryly.

We were both feeling so good, even though the sun had been eclipsed by the dark, beefy clouds and the metallic smell of rain was in the air. Actually, the absence of the sun was a good thing. The people who tromped around the cemetery were not wilting under the sun's blasting rays. If only the rain would hold off. Mr. Geyer was animated, and the crowd flocked around him, not wanting to miss a morsel of information. I was excited to see Mom and Dad caught up, too. Mom was a sucker for this history stuff, and she was putting together a story for the newspaper, but Dad is so skeptical about causes, insisting that somewhere hidden from view is a real bottom line. Yet there he was standing next to Mom, nodding encouragingly if he thought Mr. Geyer was looking his way. Dad bobbed his head like a confidante to a Puritan.

Margaret pulled out Mr. Geyer's cemetery map, the one he showed us last night that traced his tour and the tombstone stops. "Looks like he's heading to the grave site of the drowned sea captain. That's one of my favorites," she added wistfully.

I was tempted to laugh since I felt positive, and because it sounded so funny—Margaret and a favorite tombstone—but a sudden warm breeze distracted me, as it tousled my hair against my bare shoulders. I turned in the direction of the breeze.

I stared dumbly toward Prudence's grave, allowing the breeze to hit me full in the face. No one was in the west section of the cemetery, as Mr. Geyer focused on the grave sites to the east and north. All seemed still. Yet as I continued to gaze, I saw something move along the stone wall that separated our house from the cemetery. It was not really moving at first, just shimmering on top and along the side of the wall. Maybe it was those heat waves that wiggle and distort objects when you looked at them from a distance. But the sun was not out.

It was then that I realized what I was looking at, and my stomach shrank into a ball. It was the ivy. The ivy poured over the stone wall. It slithered in bunches and flowed like a babbling brook of vines. The ivy created its own path, composed of frantic plant life, from my house to something it was targeting in the west section of the cemetery among the tombstones and trees.

I grabbed Margaret's arm, pulling her attention away from the map. "Margaret," I whispered, as if the ivy might hear me, "look at the wall. Do you see the ivy?"

Margaret gasped and dropped the map. "Courtney, it's heading toward Prudence's grave."

Its vines swarmed around the earth and wrapped itself, layer upon layer, around Prudence's tombstone. Thousands of quivering leaves reminded me of bees on a hive.

"What is it doing?" I asked. "Why is the ivy covering her tombstone?" I looked over to see where Mr. Geyer and his tour might be. They were hundreds of yards away to the north. No one noticed the rivulet of ivy that was flowing from our yard.

"It must be the witch!" Margaret exclaimed. "What is she trying to tell us?" Margaret sounded angry. The tinge of frustration that I had detected in her voice last night had returned.

That is when I saw her—a woman in black. Her cape undulated in the breeze behind her. She stood beside a willow tree near Prudence's grave. One hand rested against the bark of the tree. She watched calmly as the ivy smothered the tombstone.

"Margaret," I hissed. "Do you see the witch? She's there!"

I pointed at the willow.

"I don't see her, Courtney," Margaret replied, on the verge of tears. "But I do see the ivy. Why is she doing this now? She'll ruin everything!"

I looked at the witch and then at Mr. Geyer, only separated by a few hundred yards. *The ivy is in their blood.* At least, that's what Christian's journal claimed. *How could they not see the witch?* I realized that even though Mr. Geyer was facing Prudence's grave, he was really looking into the faces of the people he believed would help save the cemetery. And their backs, including Mom's and Dad's, were to the witch.

"What should we do, Margaret?" The ivy terrified me, but another part of me thought we needed to get a closer look. Maybe then Margaret would see the witch.

But we didn't get the chance. As soon as I finished speaking, a great clap of thunder seemed to rock the ground, and I cringed at the cold, hard rain that, within moments, stung my skin and drenched my clothes.

"Oh no!" Margaret yelled, running to the posters. Yet there was no where to protect them.

I looked for Mr. Geyer and saw him hurrying the crowd, making scooping motions with his arms as if the people before him were his confused flock. The kid in the Alice Cooper T-shirt looked oblivious and was still looking around as he got caught up in the sweep of the crowd. Mom tucked her notepad under her shirt as she gave a tragic look to a willow tree that seemed to be shaking off the rain as the wind combed through its branches. Dad was hovering in back of a clutch of older ladies, who were struggling to open the compact umbrellas they kept in their purses. Everyone made a dash for their cars.

"Courtney! Margaret! Grab your posters and get in the house!" Dad yelled, suddenly at the front of the pack. His face was working its way through a series of expressions, the way it does when he gets anxious.

The witch! Could she command the rain, too?

With my soggy poster in hand, I squinted against the pelting rain toward Prudence's grave. I was unable to see the witch anywhere, and the ivy that had entwined itself around Prudence's tombstone now lay in a smoking, shriveled pile like a bouquet of flowers left too long in the sun.

Thirty minutes later, we were sitting around the kitchen table, towels draped across our shoulders. Mom poured mugs of hot chocolate, which no one made a joke about despite it being August, because we were all goose-pimpled and shivering. Dad turned off the air-conditioning as he rubbed the towel against his head. Mr. Geyer, his poofy collar flattened by the rain, stared into his cup. His glasses were fogged.

"Girls, you look like you've seen a ghost. Are you upset about the thunderstorm?" Mom asked as she took a seat and wrapped her hands around the warm mug. Her wet bangs were plastered against her forehead. When neither Margaret nor I replied, she added, "Summer thunderstorms are so unpredictable. I don't think it ruined the event, except for your beautiful posters." She looked sympathetically at the warped posterboards by the window.

I shook my head. I glanced at Margaret, her green eyes looking large in her pale face. She was staring at the ivy that lay across the window panes, trembling beneath the lashing rain.

But Mr. Geyer said it. "Jen and Tom, are you spiritual people? Do you believe in the afterlife?" He removed his glasses to wipe them with a napkin and quickly put them back on, as if to see Mom's and Dad's reactions.

Mom's eyes widened. She looked at Dad, who leaned against the kitchen counter, blowing on his mug. His short red hair looked spiked after the rubbing he gave it. Another time, I would have laughed at the look on him, but not today. Dad lowered his drink slowly to rest it on the counter.

"What do you mean?" he asked, his eyebrows rumpled the way they do when someone tries to sell him something.

"Why don't you take a seat, Tom?" Mr. Geyer suggested. His voice was as warm as the chocolate. "I want to tell you and Jen a bit more about how my daughter and I got involved with the cemetery." He looked at Margaret and smiled at her reassuringly. "Although we've known you all for only a short time, you have been good friends."

Margaret and I shot a questioning look at each other. I wondered if Mr. Geyer *had* seen the ivy or the witch in the cemetery.

Dad grabbed his mug and pulled a chair next to Mom. She patted him on his knee as she spoke. "What is it, Christian? What else do you need to tell us?" She cocked her head, truly interested. She glanced at her notepad on the kitchen counter but stayed seated.

Mr. Geyer didn't tell them everything, but he told them enough. He told them about Prudence and her missing remains, about Christian's journal and his quest to bring his daughter back to life. And he told them about the ivy that had been carved in the basement last night practically at our toes. Mom and Dad both threw me a look but allowed Mr. Geyer to continue.

"After Christian died," he finished, "that quest became a legacy for all of Christian's descendants, with one important difference. We know that we cannot bring Prudence back to life. It would be . . ." He squinted behind his glasses as if the thought hurt him. ". . . sacrilegious to even attempt such a thing, and useless in the end, as Christian is dead. That is why we are bound to unite father and daughter, not in life, but in death." Mr. Geyer paused to let this information sink in. Mom and Dad stared at him blankly. He cleared his throat to continue. "His descendants have been charged with burying them side by side. Only then can Christian and Prudence rest in peace and can their descendants live their own lives."

There was an uncomfortable silence for a moment until Dad blurted out, "You're kidding, aren't you, Christian?" Dad attempted a laugh. "It's a nice ghost story, but I don't think you need it. Your campaign—the history of the cemetery and Murmur, the stories about the stonecutters and those they carved for—is good enough. You don't want to scare people away with a tale like that. They'll think the story—"

"Farfetched?" Mr. Geyer interrupted. His voice suddenly sounded so tired. Margaret shimmied her chair closer to Mr. Geyer. Her green eyes were stern. She gave my dad a fierce look.

"This *story* is not a part of our campaign, Tom. I felt I owed you and Jennifer an explanation for recent events."

Mr. Geyer raised his chin, the same way that Margaret did when challenged. "It would be dishonest of me not to tell you our secret. Not if I call you my friends."

Then Margaret stood up. "I want to go home," she declared flatly. Her whole body trembled.

"Wait!" I yelled, pushing my chair away to stand beside her. "If you don't believe Mr. Geyer, why don't you go into the basement to see the ivy for yourself!" I couldn't tell if I sounded angry or hysterical. I didn't want my parents hurting Margaret or Mr. Geyer.

Mom stood up next. "Let's do that," she agreed.

Dad was silent, his features now a mask. He was more the scientific type, who liked to understand a theory. He shook his head. "All right. Let's go look at the basement, but I'm sure we will be able to come up with a reasonable explanation for *whatever* is down there."

Margaret and I stood shoulder to shoulder, and she held my hand as we both listened to the adults walking down the basement steps. The duration of the squeals told us that they were taking the steps slowly. We both strained to hear their conversation when the creaking stopped, but all we heard was the soft rise and fall of voices aiming to be careful.

"Look at the ivy, Courtney." Margaret pointed to the window. "Does it look to you as if it is shaking?"

Shaking, trembling. It was doing all of those things under the pounding it was taking from the rain. "I think it's just the weather, Margaret," I replied. This time. . . .

They were not down there long. We heard their weight press against the basement steps again, but this time faster. I pictured Mom taking the steps two by two.

"Courtney, why didn't you tell us about the ivy before?" Mom stood beneath the arch between the kitchen and the dining room. Her hand was splayed right above her heart. Her face was white.

I suddenly felt hot and shrugged. "I couldn't," I replied feebly. "I was worried about today."

Dad and Mr. Geyer appeared behind her. Dad ran his fingers through his wet hair, a gesture I recognized as a warning when he is frustrated. "I'm sure there is a way to explain this that takes it out of the realm of ghosts." He was almost glaring at Mr. Geyer.

Mom turned to Dad. "The ivy wasn't there yesterday morning, Tom. I was in the basement, doing the laundry." She reached for Dad's hand. "Christian, what does all this mean?" she asked. She glanced at me with one of her probing looks to make sure I was okay.

"The ivy, in whatever form it takes—plant or carving—is a sign," Mr. Geyer rushed to reassure. "It won't hurt anyone, but I don't know yet why it has appeared this way."

Dad raised his eyebrows and opened his mouth, but said nothing. He just shook his head. Mom turned around to confront Mr. Geyer.

"What or who is powering the ivy, Christian?" she asked, almost in a whisper.

"Someone who cared for Prudence and Christian, and had knowledge of the spiritual powers of nature, endowed the ivy to become the earthly manifestation of their life forces—their spirits. It's supposed to protect them where they rest and lead us to them." This time it was Mr. Geyer who stole a glance at the ivy at the window. "At least, that's my hope."

He did not mention the witch or my own personal encounters with the ivy in the woods. He raised an eyebrow at me. I passed. I was not ready to tell my story.

"Christian, I admit that the ivy carvings in the basement are a bit unusual, but do you really believe that there is some ghostly force behind them?" Dad asked. His arms were crossed now, the towel over his shoulders looking like a cape. At least he wasn't drumming his fingers the way he does when he can't hide his impatience.

"Not ghostly," Mr. Geyer corrected in a friendly tone. "But spiritual. The forces are what you might call the life energies left behind when a person moves on to the afterlife. They are a cry for help, or perhaps a clue, made by a being who has not completely given themselves up to the . . . beyond."

Mom looked intrigued and worried at the same time. She had been biting her lip while listening to Mr. Geyer and Dad. "Is that the reason you are fighting for the cemetery? Because Prudence may still be there somewhere?" she asked.

Mr. Geyer nodded slowly. "Partly. I am hoping that Prudence and Christian are buried somewhere in those grounds. I also think it is important to protect all of those who are buried there and have been resting undisturbed. That land is sacred," he added solemnly.

Margaret had tears in her eyes. She grabbed my hand under the table, making me jump in my chair.

"Courtney?" my dad asked. "What is it? Did you want to say something?"

"Yes," I said. I hoped my voice did not sound as panicked as I felt. "I think we need to help Mr. Geyer and Margaret bring Prudence and Christian together. I know I want to help. What about you, Mom?" I asked, looking her directly in the eyes.

Mom looked at Dad and then back at me. "I believed that the fight to save the cemetery was a good one from the moment Christian told me about it," she replied evenly. "I'm not as sure about what is going on in our basement, but I'm going to trust you, Christian, that whatever is happening, it is benevolent."

I flashed her a smile. "And you, Dad?" I was not ready to leave him off the hook.

He looked at us both, slowly shaking his head. "I do respect your dedication to your family's history and the history of Murmur, Christian." Dad glanced back at the basement door and scowled. "However, I'm going to have to give some thought to what you shared with us today." His face softened a little bit. "But if this search will keep that tenacious ivy from growing all over our house, then it might well be worth it."

Mr. Geyer stood and then bowed slightly, as if he were still in his Puritan role. "Margaret and I thank you for your kindness and camaraderie. I think it's time we went home now, to change into dry clothes and to begin planning our next strategy."

We all stood then and hesitated for a moment, not knowing what to say.

"Christian, do you mind if I call on you if I have a few questions about my next article?" Mom asked.

"Of course not," he replied warmly.

"And I will see you tomorrow, Courtney," Margaret said, giving me a quick hug.

I did not want to let her go. I had not had the chance

to tell Margaret about my theory that Christian and Prudence were buried somewhere near us. I hoped that she would read my mind and come looking for me tomorrow morning.

I wandered over to the kitchen window to watch the rain as Mom and Dad walked Mr. Geyer and Margaret to the door. The rain fell in ferocious slanting waves, and a ground-clinging mist hovered inches above the grass. At the edge of our yard, at the rim of the woods, the fog was thicker, I guessed because of the extra heat emitted by the bark and leaves of the trees.

Something moved along the border of the grass and trees. I saw a number of things flashing in and out of the soupy mix of mist and rain that hemmed the woods.

Only after I continued to stare did I realize that it was the cats, pacing along the edge of the woods, brushing against one another, as if in a dance. Their tails, ramrod straight, briefly relaxed to caress one another. They stopped for a moment simultaneously, to look expectantly toward our kitchen window at me. They had an impatient air about them, as if they were waiting for the thing or person that meant so much to them.

Not this time, I silently said to myself and to them.

THE MURMUR MERCURY

AUGUST 24, 2008

Special Events Feature

by Jennifer O'Brien

A tour conducted by historian Christian Geyer through the Memento Mori Cemetery this past Saturday attracted a heavy contingent of Murmur residents and visitors. The tour, cut short not by lack of interest but by unexpected rain, featured Geyer in Puritan attire and modern sensibilities. Participants were led and coaxed to peer at and touch gravestones selected for their unique art and often tragic stories the stones stoically symbolized. A number of people were heard to remark on the abundance of ivy that covered the cemetery grounds, noting that its presence was not remembered on prior visits.

chapter 11

AFTER MR. GEYER AND MARGARET WENT HOME, DAD, Mom, and I went upstairs to change our clothes. We then somehow all migrated back to the kitchen table as if it were the only safe spot in the house. Rain continued to throw itself on our roof in waves instead of drops. Thunder rolled like crashing surf.

Mom poured us a second mug of hot chocolate and we stared at the floating marshmallows as if they were tiny life preservers. For a long time, we hung out in the kitchen, me sipping loudly, trying to kill the silence. They kept looking at me, prodding me with their relentless staring to tell them something. Finally Dad caved.

"There's got to be some explanation," he said.

"You mean, beyond a hand from the grave?" Mom tried to joke but she sounded nervous. Dad didn't seem to hear her.

"You saw this ivy carving itself into the floor as you stood there, Courtney?" Dad asked gently.

I nodded. "Margaret said that it was a sign, just like Mr. Geyer said," I replied, as if that explained it all.

"I don't know what to think about Christian's story, Jen," he said to my mother, even though he was looking at me. "I mean, they're nice people and the cause is a good one, but doesn't this all sound like an episode from *Tales from the Dark Side* or something?" He sighed heavily and ran his hand through his red hair. He obviously had not bothered to comb it while he was upstairs.

Mom paused thoughtfully. She was wearing her comfortable pink robe. "I don't know, Tom," she said slowly, using her finger to push a marshmallow below the surface. "Sometimes I get a funny feeling in this house. I will be doing the dishes and I get the weird sensation of somebody watching me. Then I turn around and all I see is that ivy." She stopped to stare at it, now plastered against the window. "Of course it sounds crazy, but how do we explain the new growth of *carved* ivy in the basement? It wasn't there yesterday morning."

My eyes darted between my mom's and dad's faces as if I were watching a tennis match. It was Dad's turn and he was frowning.

"I don't know how to explain it, but surely there *is* an explanation. Maybe it's some sort of mold," he offered weakly.

"That chisels itself into walls and floors?" I asked sarcastically, unable to help myself.

Dad gave me the evil eye. "I know it sounds far-fetched, Courtney, but until we have a good explanation, I don't want you going into the basement, okay?" His face softened with concern, and I felt bad.

"I was just kidding you, Dad. Don't worry. I'm not going down there without you guys."

Mom sighed heavily. "Okay. Let's tackle one challenge at a time. I still think we'll have a good cemetery story. People seemed really interested during the tour. So first thing tomorrow I'm going to write the story and get those photos developed. Right now, it's all a jumble in my mind." She cleared her throat. "I think I need to put a little time between my article and what Christian shared with us this afternoon." She smiled. "How about we go into town for dinner tonight? I know I could use the change."

Dad and I nodded our agreement. It would be nice to join the present for a little while. If nothing else, downtown Murmur at least would look *normal* on a Saturday night.

It had finally stopped raining and we ate dinner at one of the Main Street sidewalk cafes that blossomed like dandelions in the good weather. That was Dad's simile, as he did not like

to eat his dinner *outdoors*, unless it was a barbecue. For
that reason the tables and chairs that sprang up along the
sidewalk reminded him of those cheerful weeds. Mom and
I loved cafes, though, and marveled how even Murmur,
Massachusetts, could look like Paris on a warm summer
night. The sidewalks and curbs were crowded with people
flowing in and out of stores or simply sitting on the curbs
with a coffee or soda in hand. The streetlamps provided a
soft light to the thick summer air. Although this was small-
town America, as Dad liked to point out, here on Main
Street the witch and her ivy seemed worlds away.

I did not get that nervous tickle in my stomach again
until we got home. Mom tried to scoot me right up
the stairs, but not before I saw Dad draw the latch on the
basement door. For some reason, that made me all
the more nervous, because I expected Dad to not take any
of this seriously. I wanted him to scoff at the notion of
spirits and ivy.

Even as I lay in bed, watching my ceiling fan hypnoti-
cally whir and wobble above my head, I was unable to
relax. In the darkness of my room, the day's events unfolded
before my eyes, saving me the trouble of having to dream.
And although I did not want to relive the basement scene,
I saw in my mind that ivy budding on the basement ceiling and floor.

I must have fallen asleep, because when I woke, I heard the clock in the hallway chiming one. And then I heard what sounded like humming somewhere outside my bedroom window. A girl's voice was sliding up and down a tune I did not recognize.

I tugged on the sheet, turning over so that I was facing the window. I listened harder and only heard the crickets, a sound I always found comforting in the middle of the night. Then it came again, weaving in and out of the crickets' rhythmic breathing. I sat up slightly, still drowsy. The humming grew louder.

My heart began to speed up. I got out of bed, walked the few feet to my window, and sat on the ledge. I peered down into the yard at the grass glowing softly in the moonlight. Beyond, the cemetery spread out as if it were infinite, replacing all homes, roads, and fields. The tombstones gleamed like macabre night-lights, simultaneously inviting and warning all who dared to both enter and stay away. The humming became faint again but I could still detect it. Where was that sound coming from? Was it coming from the woods?

I realized I was trembling and felt the hair on the back of my neck prickle. Then a thin figure dressed in white with long sleeves and a long, billowy skirt hopped over the cemetery wall into our yard. Without looking back, she ran to the shed and stopped.

My mouth moved but no sound came out. I wanted to step back from the window but felt my nose pressing against the screen. I watched her dart to the edge of the woods, standing on tiptoe as if she could see into the darkness. She acted as if she were playing hide-and-seek with herself at a frantic pace. The tune she hummed sped up when she did and slowed when she stopped to inspect the grounds around her. Then she dashed across the yard to our basement window, stopping to drop to her hands and knees to peer in.

And then she looked up, as if she could feel my eyes following her every movement.

This time I did cry out at the sight of the face looking up at me. It was a girl about my age with black hair pulled into a bun and piercing green eyes. She looked like Margaret, or as Margaret would have looked if she dressed like a Puritan. Her face was thinner, whiter, and more angled than Margaret's.

"Prudence?" I called out, my heart banging so hard that I had to grab hold of the windowsill to keep my balance.

She cocked her head at me and stared, squinting at first until her face softened into a smile. She raised her arms to me like a little kid does to her parents when she is tired of walking.

As Prudence stood in the yard, I thought I saw another movement behind the shed, but I was not sure. It was so dark and the shed was shielded even from the moonlight by the trees. It was like a shadow skirting along the edges of our yard, keeping within the blackness of the tree canopy. Then the witch stepped into the moonlight.

She took her time approaching Prudence. I watched, fascinated, as the soft summer breeze played with the long tendrils of the witch's unbound hair. She gripped the edges of her cape with both hands. I was afraid that she would look up at me, but she only had eyes for Prudence.

Prudence was standing directly below my window, as if expecting me to lower a sheet to hoist her up. The witch walked faster. Her eyes shone like a cat's in the moonlight.

"Prudence!" I screamed as the witch suddenly reached out to grab her. It was then that Prudence disappeared, her body shimmered into dust touched by moonbeams. The witch looked up at me then and released her cape so that it flapped like crows' wings behind her. I pushed myself away from the window and nearly fell against my bedroom door. I had to tell Mom and Dad.

The hallway darkness was only slightly tinged by the weak light of the lamp on the table at the bottom of the stairs. I grabbed the newel post on the banister at the top of the stairs, using it to steady myself as I tried to slow my breathing. I listened to the air. I could not hear the humming now, but instead heard a faint tapping coming from downstairs—a sharp, incessant, steady tap like a hammer hitting concrete. I knew that sound. I felt as if somebody was squeezing my heart in their hand like a bird's egg. It was the chiseling.

I do not know why I went down the steps instead of bursting into my parents' bedroom. One part of me screamed from inside not to go down there, but another part felt a tug from something else. It was not terrifying but gentle and needy, as it led me to the front landing. The chiseling was louder and more frantic now. I turned to look at the basement door, the best-lit feature of the house, thanks to that table lamp squeezed between it and the stairway. I drew the latch and opened the door. I nearly fell back from the force of what sounded like hundreds of hammers and chisels, the metallic clanking buffeting my eardrums.

"Prudence?" I whispered, although whatever drew me here told me it was not Prudence. I clicked on the basement light, but the chiseling did not stop. I figured that since I did not scare it the first time, it would not be afraid of me now. I walked down a few steps, bending to peer into the belly of the basement. The sound, magnified to a deafening roar, vibrated off of the walls and floors and pounded against my body in frantic waves. The basement door closed behind me.

I stood on the steps, my muscles frozen, the fear beginning to swell in my stomach. More than anyone else, I wanted Margaret by my side. *The witch won't hurt us. She is just trying to tell us something.* I repeated Margaret's words. *What would Margaret do if she were with me?* I knew she would walk to the center of the basement, and look the ivy chiseled or real, right in the eye.

The plaster walls and slate floor were ringing as I slowly edged toward the center of the room. This time, every exposed surface that I looked at—walls, ceiling, floor—was covered with the intricate, dizzying patterns of ivy vines. I covered my ears with my hands as I looked around the room, spying little puffs of plaster dust where a new ivy leaf was suddenly appearing. Yet I was unafraid. The presence that I felt in the basement seemed friendly, like it wanted to share a secret. I remembered the ivy connected Prudence and Christian. At least that was what the witch told Christian, according to his journal.

"What is it?" I whispered, trying to understand. "What do you want me to know?" My teeth chattered as I asked the question, not daring to shout above the ringing of invisible chisels hitting stone and their echoes colliding against one another.

Then the chiseling stopped. My ears stung slightly from the noise. I suddenly could hear footsteps on the floor above me and the basement doorknob jiggling in its socket. My attention was pulled back to the center floor, where a tiny chiseling sound began tapping a new shape into the slate that was already crammed with ivy. The tapping was slower this time, and the strike of the hammer chipped deeper into the slate. I felt a sudden chill and hugged myself as the new carving was completed. It formed a simple *P*. It reminded me of Sleeping Beauty, protected and hidden by monstrous thornbushes for all those years. Suddenly I wanted to shout. *I understood!*

"Mom!" I yelled instead as I saw her crouched outside the basement window, a flashlight in her hand. Her face looked contorted as she pressed it against the dirty pane. The light from her flashlight seemed to ricochet all over the room in her unsteady hand.

"Courtney!" I could hear her yell against the thick glass of the windows. "Are you all right?"

I nodded yes as I noticed that she was in her summer pajamas. Was the witch still out there? I motioned to her to come back into the house.

Behind me the basement door slammed open and Dad yelled my name with much more gusto than needed. He pounded down the steps and looked wildly around the room. His hair was sticking up in all sorts of directions and one cheek still had a pillow line slanting across it. He scooped me up as we met at the bottom of the stairs.

"Courtney, are you okay? I couldn't get that basement door open!" He yelled it almost accusingly.

"Dad, I'm fine, really," I rushed to assure him.

Mr. Geyer stood at the top of the steps. He wiped his forehead with a handkerchief and gave me a big smile. I suddenly felt way too happy for this hour of the morning.

"Mr. Geyer!" I called, peering around Dad. "I know where Prudence is!"

Prudence.

noun. Fourteenth century.
1 : displaying wisdom discretion, caution, carefulness;
2 : common sense, canniness;
3 : uses foresight or forethought;
4 : providence.

chapter 12

I WONDERED HOW THE KITCHEN TABLE BECAME THE CENTER of our life, for there we all sat again, this time with a hot cup of tea. Mom was in her pajamas, grass stains on her knees. Dad and Mr. Geyer were in baggy shorts and T-shirts. Only Margaret was dressed for a new day, her shorts and shirt without a wrinkle. I had fallen asleep in yesterday's clothes.

I leaned across the table, my gaze swerving back and forth between Mr. Geyer's and Margaret's faces. Margaret said she had a dream about me being locked in the basement. I kept calling her name. That was why they were here in the middle of the night. Now they looked at me expectantly.

"Prudence is here," I said excitedly. "She is buried in the basement."

Mr. Geyer sat up straight. Mom and Dad stiffened.

"I don't understand any of this," Mom complained. "All I know is that I had the scare of my life when I heard all that noise and discovered you locked in the basement." She turned to my dad. "Tom, we have to get Courtney away from here."

Mr. Geyer opened his mouth to speak, but held back. Margaret shook her head back and forth slowly. "It's okay," she offered gently. "Listen to Courtney."

Dad stared at Margaret and pushed his mug away. "Jen is right. Nothing makes sense. For a little while tonight, this house was inhabited by something unnatural." He grabbed for my mom's hand. "And I don't even *believe* in this sort of thing."

"Dad," I interrupted. "It's okay." I said it sincerely, because ever since I felt that presence, I also felt a reassuring friendliness—it was happy to see us here. "That *something* that you are talking about, I felt it, too, when I was in the basement. It was chiseling more ivy and the letter *P* into the floor."

"*P?*" Mr. Geyer repeated, his voice trembling slightly.

I had not had the chance to show Mr. Geyer the chiseler's latest work. Dad had rushed me up the basement stairs and slammed and locked the door behind us.

"Yes." I thought for a moment about telling them how I saw Prudence prancing around our yard, but decided to hold that part of the story until later. "It was like the thing that was guiding the chiseling was trying to pound me over the head with the idea that Prudence is buried here, in this house."

"So the witch was trying to help us find her! The ivy was like a trail of bread crumbs!" Margaret's eyes were shining with emotion. Even the tips of her ears were tinged with color. She turned and placed a hand on Mr. Geyer's knee. "Isn't this wonderful, Dad? Courtney may have found her!"

Dad and Mom had been mute with shock during this part of the conversation. Dad broke out of the daze first.

"Courtney, I can reliably say now that anything is possible, but are you suggesting that we remove the slate from the basement floor and look for Prudence's bones?" Dad's voice cracked under the strain of even asking such a question.

"Well, not exactly," I replied. "I think maybe her coffin is there. For some reason I get the feeling that whoever moved her did it to keep Prudence close—and safe."

Mr. Geyer was nodding. "I suspect Christian may have had a part in Prudence's relocation." He took off his glasses and cleaned them with the hem of his shirt.

Margaret turned to my mom and placed her hand gently on her wrist and asked breathlessly, "Would you mind if we look?"

My mother shrugged, looking at my dad as she always did when she wanted to include him in a decision. "I don't see why not." She glanced at the clock hanging above the stove. "It might be three in the morning, but I can't imagine going back to bed tonight." She tilted her head, awaiting Dad's response. He stifled a yawn.

"I've got a crowbar and some shovels in the shed," he announced. Despite the resignation in his voice, Dad was a man of action. I knew he wanted more than anything to figure out what was going on.

The basement bulbs cast shadows under our eyes, making us all look like vampires, except for Mr. Geyer, of course. His super lenses caught the weak light as it glowed from the various points on the basement ceiling, so that Mr. Geyer became another source of illumination. Mom held the flashlight in her hand and kept looking nervously around the room for any weird activity.

Mr. Geyer and Margaret were on their knees, their fingers probing the carvings in the slate slabs as if they were reading Braille. Margaret turned to look at me.

"Courtney, this is amazing," she said, her voice a trembling whisper. "She let you witness this?" She extended her hand as if she wanted me to kneel beside her.

I followed her lead, laying my palms flat against the surface of the chiseled slab. The roughness of the stone and the carvings almost tickled.

"Courtney," my mom said nervously behind me. "Please get up."

I turned to her, as Margaret turned to me. "It's okay, Mom. It's so weird, but I don't feel at all scared or freaked out. I don't sense anything bad here, just . . . a feeling like a sigh of relief."

My dad frowned, probably getting a little itchy because he still held a crowbar and shovel in his hands and had not used them.

Mr. Geyer leaned on one knee to stand up. "I'm sorry, Tom. Margaret and I have never witnessed such a manifestation. I'm literally shaking. Can you feel the presence?" he asked hopefully.

Margaret nodded.

"I can," I confirmed. "It feels like something is embracing us, encouraging us to keep going, as if we are part of some incredible journey."

Mom put her arm around my shoulder and pulled me against her as Mr. Geyer smiled. "Courtney is incredibly sensitive. A truly remarkable girl," he said, gently resting his hand on the top of my head.

Dad cleared his throat. "Shall we get started?"

"Certainly. A splendid idea," Mr. Geyer replied. His voice sounded a little higher than normal.

Mom, Margaret, and I stepped back and grasped one another's hands as Dad pried the edges of the slate floor that contained the fury of carvings superimposed with the large, ornate *P*.

I looked around the room, peering past the dark corners of the basement, the pile of boxes in the center, and the washer and dryer on the other side. I wanted to make sure that the ivy was okay with what we were doing. There was no new chiseling or real ivy squirming across the basement floor trying to stop us. I took a deep breath. We must be doing the right thing.

The three of us remained silent as Dad and Mr. Geyer squatted to pull up the first loosened slab. They grunted at its weight as they lay it gently aside. A puff of cool air tinged with the aroma of damp earth pressed gently against my face. No one spoke a word to one another as they removed three more. Each slab was the size of a tombstone.

The dirt beneath the slate stones was soft and red. Dad and Mr. Geyer shoveled easily and carefully. Neat piles of dirt began growing beside them both. I was mesmerized. With each new shovelful of dirt removed, I felt my stomach tighten until it felt like the size of a hard little ball.

Mr. Geyer's shovel suddenly thumped in the dirt.

"You hit something!" Margaret announced, letting go of my hand to peer into the three-foot hole they had dug.

Bits of stone and gravel embedded in the earthen walls sparkled when they caught the light.

"Yes," Mr. Geyer agreed. He tapped his shovel gently along the length of the hole. The blade of the shovel continued to thump along the top of something still covered by a layer of dirt. Mr. Geyer looked expectantly at Dad.

Dad nodded. "Okay, let's dig around the edges. Looks like it's about six feet long and two and a half feet wide."

I was holding my breath now. Mom twisted her head back and forth, one hand periodically covering her mouth as if to hold something back. Margaret cried silently, but her shoulders heaved at the effort, as Dad and Mr. Geyer unearthed what appeared to be a wooden box. Its lid was splintered and stained dark by the damp earth.

"Is it her coffin?" Mom ventured, pulling me forward with her as she still held my hand.

"I think so," Mr. Geyer replied softly. "But we must remove the lid to be sure."

Dad did not look so sure. He wiped the sweat from his forehead with the back of his hand, leaving a dirt streak that looked like an exercise band. "You really want to take the top off?" he asked.

Mr. Geyer nodded solemnly. "We have to. This may simply contain Christian's carving tools. He noted in his journal that he buried them sometime after Prudence's death. He refused to carve another stone after he completed hers."

Dad sighed and turned to us girls. "Okay. Do you all want to wait upstairs while Christian and I inspect this box?" His question sounded more like a command.

"No," Mom answered while my mouth was still forming the same reply. "I mean, we have witnessed this much. I think we need to see it now to its finish."

"Thank you, Mrs. O'Brien," Margaret said gratefully.

Dad frowned but took his crowbar to the box's lid, which squeaked in protest as he pried along its edges. The wood looked very old and flimsy, nestled in the dirt. It reminded me of an ancient trapdoor to a secret passageway into the earth.

A few of its nails simply cracked as sections of the once-smooth wood split apart as Dad crouched to press all of his weight against the crowbar. He moved awkwardly around the perimeter of the hole, carefully prying along the lid's edges little by little. After a few passes, the wood made a popping sound as if the box suddenly cast it off. A more powerful smell of earth, dust, and metal perfumed the air.

Dad lifted the wooden lid and slid it behind him across the basement floor. We held on to one another as we leaned over the hole to peer into the box.

"Thank God," Mr. Geyer pronounced, grabbing hold of Margaret and pulling her head into his chest. For nestled in the box on top of a yellowed and fraying quilt lay Prudence. Instead of stepping back in horror, I felt a weird relief, simply glad that Prudence was finally safe and sound. I knew it was Prudence, because the bones held crumbling pieces of the loose white skirt and shirt that I had just seen her wearing as she had raced around our backyard. Of course, the clothes looked much older, were faded and torn, but I could still recognize them. At her feet were a collection of tools—chisels, hammers, and stones. The small stones were the color and texture of slate.

Mom and Dad were silent and stepped back as Margaret and Mr. Geyer knelt beside the hole. His hand trembled as he held it over the coffin, almost as if he were giving a blessing.

"Dad, you must touch her and then you must touch me, remember?" Margaret prodded him. Her gaze was focused on the coffin as she took his hand to guide it toward the place where Prudence's heart once beat. Before he did so, he leaned into the hole to gently pull at the edges of the quilt, as if to make sure that Prudence was comfortable.

Mom and Dad stepped back and hovered behind me. Both were wide-eyed.

I watched Mr. Geyer as a tear traveled down his cheek.

He turned to Margaret, still holding her hand. "We must find Christian," he said roughly.

It was then that I saw what looked like an old rolled-up paper sticking out from the small pile of stones at Prudence's feet. "What is that?" I pointed into the coffin. We all leaned in now as Mr. Geyer carefully plucked the paper from what I guessed to be remnants of a tombstone.

"It looks like a parchment," Mom murmured, no longer able to contain herself.

Mr. Geyer stumbled to his feet as he clutched the scrolled paper. He opened it and whispered, "It's a page from Christian's journal."

"Read it to us," Margaret said, suddenly clasping my hand.

He wiped his cheek with the back of his wrist and straightened, as if assuming the old Puritan stance. His voice went low as he read.

The witch said that this was the only way to end our misery.

I knew she loved me. I never doubted her word on that.

She had refused to be my wife because she was a witch.

But she was unafraid to have my child.
Prudence.
Your mother knows what to do.
"Bury her," she said, "in the cellar.
Bury her at your foundation.
They cannot hurt her there.
And when you die," she promised, "I
will bury you,
Not far from me or our daughter.
In the end, the ivy will bind us,
And in time, unite us for eternity.
The ivy will know when the time is right."
God help me for believing her.

I wondered if everyone's heart beat as ferociously as mine.

"What does it mean?" I whispered. Even Dad leaned into our circle now. Mr. Geyer was trembling. He cleared his throat before replying.

"It means that the witch had planned all this, as if somehow she could manipulate nature's laws to bring them all together in the future." He took off his glasses and rubbed the lenses against his shirt. "Together in a time when witches would no longer be burned at the stake."

Margaret's emerald eyes seemed to eclipse her face. She looked at Mr. Geyer. Her lips moved as if to speak, but the words seemed lost to her. Mr. Geyer gently tilted her face toward his own, scrutinizing it as if she were a stranger.

"I never guessed that Prudence was also the witch's daughter," he said in a whisper. He shook his head.

Dad and Mom had moved to the toe of the excavation. Mom had placed one hand protectively against her belly, which was a nervous habit I recognized. Usually I like to joke with her about her fear of "spilling her guts," but not today. Dad pulled his T-shirt up to wipe his face, a gesture that would usually inspire fury in Mom, but she only had eyes for the coffin in the ground. Dad dropped the crowbar and grabbed for Mom's hand.

"Does this mean that Prudence was never buried in the cemetery at all?" Mom asked, her face pinched with concern.

Mr. Geyer shook his head and paused, as if mentally putting the pieces together. "No. Prudence was indeed buried in the cemetery. We found records to confirm it. That is why we've been searching. . . ." He trailed off and turned to look at Margaret. "Christian dug her up and buried her here, at the witch's beckoning. The witch seemed to fear that the townspeople might desecrate her grave."

I thought of the scene I had witnessed from my window only a few hours ago. Prudence skipped about the yard, while the witch lurked in the trees behind her. The witch must have been reaching out to Prudence, not menacing her. The mother was begging her daughter to come to her, like a naughty kid.

I looked back at Margaret. "You look like Prudence," I mumbled. Margaret cocked her head at me and smiled as if to say, *Hmmmm?*

And then Mr. Geyer stepped between us to address Mom and Dad. "If you don't mind, Jen and Tom, when the time is appropriate, I would like to bury Prudence in the woods by her father."

"Do you know where *he* is buried?" my dad asked. "We'd be glad to assist with reuniting your family." Mom glanced up to give him a quick smile.

As Mr. Geyer hesitated, I heard my own voice pipe in.

"I know where Christian is buried," I announced slowly, because the revelation had only just dawned. All faces turned to me. "I saw the witch in the woods, placing ivy around a plot of ground. I can show you where this is." I noticed the now shocked looks from Mom and Dad.

"What do you mean you saw the witch, Courtney?" Dad asked, horrified.

"Courtney, you are a blessing," Mr. Geyer said warmly, as if he did not hear Dad. "I would be much obliged if you could lead us to this plot in the morning. Right now, we've all got to get some rest."

She appears at all hours, leaving a bouquet, or when she is feeling less generous, a sprig of ivy behind. I have found the vine on my front steps, along the path to the house, in the frozen, dead plot of land where Prudence and I grew our herbs. Although it is winter, the ivy she leaves is vibrant and green as if newly grown. It does not bear the burnished, faded color of the ivy vines that cling to my house over the cold, dark months.

Her ivy appears ageless, everlasting. I yearn for Prudence.

—Christian Geyer

chapter 13

LATER THAT MORNING WE WERE UP AT DAWN, UNABLE
to sleep after we had found Prudence's grave.

We were at our kitchen table when we saw Mr.
Geyer and Margaret standing in our backyard. Wisps of fog
clung like cobwebs to the tree branches and lay across the
grass in clumps of dew. Margaret had her hair in braids and
was wearing her white tennis sneakers. I worried how dirty
they would get as we tromped through the woods to
Christian's grave. She must have seen us staring dumbly
through the kitchen window because she gave me a shy
little wave.

Mr. Geyer did a sort of funny bow. He looked pleased
as he stood there in one of his many checkered-shirts-and-
baggy-shorts ensembles. His knees looked knobby from the
distance. For a moment I thought I might cry. He suddenly
looked so vulnerable.

Dad broke the silence. "Is this legal what we're doing?"

he asked, leaning over his black cup of coffee. His face looked scrubbed, absent of the mixture of dirt and sweat that it bore last night. "I mean, we're digging up a body and burying it in the woods. Are we supposed to call the police or something?"

Before I could respond, Mom made some impatient noise. "Of course it's legal. This is what they want." Her lips pursed in trying to name them. "Prudence isn't supposed to be in our basement anyway." She shrugged.

"Well, she's not supposed to be in the woods either," Dad replied. He glanced at Mr. Geyer and Margaret. "I feel like last night was a dream," he said, his voice tinged with worry. "I mean," he almost stammered, "are these people for real?"

"Of course they're for real!" I exploded, suddenly feeling a bit panicky, but for a moment I saw them through Dad's eyes. A strange, nerdy guy and his beautiful, enchanting daughter, enveloped in the soft gray mist. They had moved to the fringe of the woods and lost their color to the fog. Their forms blurred into the tree mist. Mr. Geyer had his arm protectively around Margaret's slight shoulders as they peered into the shadows that still clung to the trees. "They may be a little different," I said fiercely, "but they're my friends."

"Courtney's right, Tom." Mom's eyes looked wet as she

brushed her hair from her forehead. "They're certainly not your typical neighbors, but I can sense the goodness in them." She pushed her mug of coffee to the center of the table. "They're fulfilling a family pledge made centuries ago. I have to admire them." Her voice was filled with emotion.

Dad looked ashamed. He stood up. "Okay, can I help it if I'm not as sensitive as you two? I'm not supposed to be, right? I'm a guy." He shrugged and waited for our smiles. Mom drummed her fingers against the table.

"All right. I know when I'm beaten." He looked toward the Geyers and motioned that we would be just a minute. "Let's go, you two. We have a coffin to bury."

I led the way, anxious to retrace the route that I had fled the other day. Margaret was right behind me but hardly made a sound, except when she politely whispered a warning to be careful as she held a branch to keep it from swatting my mother in the face. I could hear my mom and dad breathing heavily, as much of the hike required a fair amount of crouching and ducking to get through the trees that had long ago reclaimed the path. And although it was not yet seven o'clock, the rain that had pounded the woods last night seemed to cling to the air. The ground and leaves were wet, and breathing too much air made you feel as if you were drowning. When we reached the massive tree and clearing, we all staggered from the path, soaked by our sweat and the dew.

Fog washed across the old tree roots, which bulged from the earth like tiny mountains. The bark of the huge tree was still black from the penetrating rain. And the ivy carved into its trunk looked as if it had been drawn with ink. I gazed at the plot of ground that the witch had bordered with her vine. Some of the plant had washed away from the plot and lay tangled in clumps like seaweed left behind by the tide. Yet a few strands remained bravely where the witch had placed them.

"Look, Dad." Margaret pointed beyond the tree, into a section of woods that was dark with growth. It was there that I had seen the witch disappear after laying her ivy bouquet.

We heard the mewing of the cats before we saw them. Their chorus, composed of individual pleas for food and attention, grew stronger as they approached. Ten cats emerged from the wood's scrubby undergrowth to circle the tree—tabbies, tigers, white, and black—all stared at us expectantly with their luminous eyes. They sat creating

their own feline border around Christian's plot and their tails swished nervously.

"Our cats," Mr. Geyer said calmly. His hair was plastered to his forehead with sweat. His lenses were steamed. "I wondered where they had gone. They look well fed and cared for," he added with relief.

"Your cats?" Dad echoed, his voice cracking. Dad's T-shirt was soaked and the bags under his eyes were a sure sign that he would be cranky. Dad did not function well with little sleep. "Does that mean that this is the spot, then?"

Margaret was squinting at the cats with suspicion. "Why didn't they ever lead us here?" she asked. Her tone sounded hurt. "I took such good care of them. I talked to them all the time. They knew what we were looking for."

Mom laid her hand lightly on Margaret's shoulder and playfully fingered her braid. Mom's other hand was on Dad's arm, fortifying his depleted spirit. "Cats have their own code, Margaret. They do things in their own time," she explained. "But it looks to me that they are telling us that we have found Christian's grave, just as Courtney promised."

Mr. Geyer clasped my shoulder affectionately. "Look there, girls, by that old, dwarfed fir tree that seems to be bowing under the weight of this tiny forest."

I looked at the tree whose roots straddled the clearing and the swath of woods. Against its wizened trunk leaned an old black shovel. The witch had finally grown impatient.

It was four that afternoon when Mom poked her head into my room. She was wearing a sleeveless shirt and a pair of shorts. Her hair was pulled back with barrettes that made her look like a little kid.

"I couldn't sleep." She smiled easily from the doorway. "How about you?"

Propped against my pillow, I had a book in my hands—*The Witch of Blackbird Pond*—so I guess my answer was obvious. It was one of my favorites and I thought that the research could not hurt.

"Mom, I don't get it. I don't understand how the witch created this magic ivy or how she could have been waiting here for all these centuries. How did she become a witch and learn how to do these things?" I sat up in bed and closed my book. I kept thinking about last night, when the witch appeared in the yard to reclaim Prudence.

Mom shrugged and walked slowly to my bed, gently sitting on the edge. She pushed the hair off my forehead with her hand. "I don't know, Courtney. There's no easy answer." She looked out the window. We both did. It was oddly gray and quiet. "We'd probably have to go back in time and experience the witch's life to understand why and how she learned the things she did."

I was unsatisfied. "Why do you think she burned down the house after Christian buried Prudence in the basement?" I was sure that the witch had done it. She was the reason for everything strange that had happened.

Mom cocked her head before she answered, as if she were thinking something through. "If the witch did set fire to the house, maybe it was because of what she knew people believed. I think she was trying to erase all evidence that Prudence or Christian had been there, to protect them." Mom reached for my hand and rubbed it between her own, as if to make sure that I was flesh and blood.

"Back in the time when witches were burned at the stake, people were accused of being witches simply for being different. And everyone was so afraid about surviving in this new land. Fear always feeds superstitions. Perhaps Prudence's mother was simply an independent, special woman. From what you and the Geyers have told me, she sounded very spiritual, but her beliefs were grounded in God's presence in the natural world, it seems."

I nodded and smiled. It was a nice answer, but it still

did not explain many things. "But how come she didn't die like they did?"

She bit her lip while combing out my hair with her fingers. "Who said she didn't die? Perhaps she just has a feisty spirit." She looked into my eyes and smiled. "She obviously loved Christian and Prudence very much. To think what could be if all of us had the ability to make our love span a few centuries. I think that was, or is, the witch's real power."

I smiled, not knowing what else to say. "I can't sleep, either," I finally replied.

"I knew that." Mom laughed. "That's why I came by to see if you wanted to go for a walk."

"Can we?" I sat up straight. Trying to make yourself sleep can be really tiring. "How about Dad?" I asked.

"Sleeping like a baby." She smiled sarcastically. "All of that moaning about being in the midst of the unexplainable, and as soon as his head hit the pillow he was out."

Mom stood up and walked to the window. She bent to pick up my sneakers and swung them lightly by their laces.

"Where are we going to walk?" I asked.

She turned from the window. "Why, through the cemetery, of course. I need to start thinking about an angle for my next story."

I'm happy, too,
because Dad promises that
I will see you again.
And that you will recognize me.
For now, the cats will be our bond.

Care for them for me.
Our mission is done.

chapter 14

WE BURIED PRUDENCE NEXT TO CHRISTIAN AND placed our own ivy border around both plots. As we did so, the cats were all over us, rubbing up against our legs and ducking under our arms as we kneeled on the soft ground to place our ivy wreaths. The orange cat kept sticking its tail under my nose and I tried to shoo it away.

"Courtney, he's thanking you! Don't be so rude," Margaret had scolded with a big smile on her face. I remember thinking how radiant she looked as she kind of glowed in a beam of sunlight that had penetrated the leaves of our tree. "And he's my favorite. I want you to take special care of him."

I glanced up, not quite catching Margaret's meaning. She turned away before I could see her eyes.

When we had finished laying the ivy, Dad had asked about getting a metal plaque or stone marker, with an

inscription that noted that Prudence and Christian were
buried here.

"That won't be necessary, Tom," Mr. Geyer said gently.
Both of their shirts were soaked in sweat. "I'd rather that
we not bring any undue attention to this site. Let's concen-
trate our efforts on the preservation of the cemetery."

"Just what would you like us to do, Christian?" Mom
asked, brushing her hands together. "I took a walk through
the cemetery. In the quiet, it felt so sacred there, something
I didn't sense during our tour."

Mr. Geyer nodded solemnly. "Yes. I know what you
mean. The spirits of the living are stronger than the spirits
of the dead. Our little crowd was a rambunctious one, too,"
he added with a smile. "Until the rain chased us all away."

"Is that bad?" I asked. I thought of the sentinel ivy,
Mom's phrase for it, that seemed to watch over the cemetery.

Margaret slipped her arm around Mr. Geyer's back as he
rubbed his chin thoughtfully. Mom and I stood before
them, waiting expectantly for his answer. Dad was over by
the tree, collecting our shovels. He banged two of them
together to loosen the moist dirt that still clung to the
metal. The sound was jarring. Mom threw Dad a "be quiet"
look as he shrugged his shoulders.

"No, no," Mr. Geyer replied. His eyes were warm and
earnest and, for a moment, looked moist behind his glasses.

"No, Courtney. It's very important that you bring the living to the cemetery. The living are the only ones who can protect the dead." He removed his glasses and used his shirt to clean the lenses.

Mom tilted her head, as if waiting for Mr. Geyer to continue. "Would you like us to help you with the tours?" Mom asked, unable to remain silent any longer. "And I would be more than happy to continue to write about the cemetery. The history is fascinating."

Mr. Geyer smiled gratefully. "That would be wonderful." Then he turned to look directly at me. "Margaret and I are going to rely on you both more than you can imagine."

What did that mean? But before I could ask, Dad swaggered over to us with the shovels thrown over his shoulder like he did this work all the time.

"Ready to head home?" Dad asked. "Looks like we all could use something cold to drink."

We all nodded silently. I guess it was at that moment that we sort of promised to remain forever mute about the burial plot in the woods.

The following day was clear and beautiful, the sun casting

the day in a warm, golden glow. It was already ten o'clock when I skipped out the front door to visit Margaret and Mr. Geyer. As I walked down the driveway, I turned to look at our house. It looked raw and clean as if the rain had given its walls a good scrubbing. Then I felt my jaw drop. Some of the ivy was gone. Until now, it had covered our house like a soft green curtain. Dad had joked that perhaps in the winter we would actually see our house beneath its muted leaves, but now the ivy seemed to have parted from the center of the walls like a curtain opening on a stage.

I ran back to check the front and side gardens for the vines of ivy that curled and serpentined through my mother's begonias and mums. The ivy was still there, but like the walls of the house, it seemed to creep back in retreat. The flowers in the center of the beds were suddenly unadorned by ivy.

How could those millions of vines and leaves that only yesterday had clung to our house through that pelting rainstorm suddenly lose their grip?

I raced down our driveway and turned to run clumsily through the soggy, marshy swale alongside the road. I had to tell Margaret and Mr. Geyer about this latest development. Was this a good thing that the ivy was letting go? I was finally getting used to its stubborn presence. When we first moved here, the ivy had felt menacing, as if it were watching my every move. Now I deemed it more a nosy neighbor that kept its eye on everything because it cared.

I ignored the cars that honked at me as they passed and I barely noticed the sweet smell of the saturated cornstalks. As I neared the path that lead to the Geyers' stone cabin, I suddenly felt panicked.

I slowed to a trot when I touched the path, for a new doubt gnawed at my stomach as I recalled the vague comments that Margaret had made about us helping with the cemetery tours and her cats. *Why would she say such things?*

I felt my feet press softly into the carpet of pine needles that covered the dirt. I welcomed the sudden coolness of the woods. My ten-minute run had wet my bangs and the back of my shirt. I listened for their voices as I turned the tiny bend and saw their house. Its door was open slightly. Its windows shaded. The cat tins that were lined in a neat row along the front of the house were empty. I whimpered before I could stop myself. My heart felt like it was stuck in my throat.

I must have stood in front of the door for at least five minutes before I worked up the nerve to push it open. While waiting, I called for Margaret and Mr. Geyer. My voice sounded much higher than normal to me. I listened to the noisy chatter of the birds that must have been perched wing to wing on the branches of the trees surrounding the house. Were they talking to me? "Go on in, go on in, go on in," they seemed to be chirping.

The house felt cool and lonely. I glanced to my right into the living room. All of the rental-house furniture was exactly as I had last seen it. The couch, the armchairs, and the coffee table were not far from the fireplace, but nothing seemed to bear the impression of the Geyers' touch.

The dining room was in front of me. The plain pine table that had previously been smothered with stacks of papers, photos, and clippings was bare except for a letter-size white envelope placed precisely in its center beside Christian's journal.

I crept like a burglar toward them, until I could plainly read my name written in Margaret's sweeping script. "Oh no," I whispered. "Margaret," I pleaded as I plucked the envelope from the table and opened it as if my touch might cause it to disintegrate.

Dear Courtney,

I'm so glad I met you. Dad says that you saved us because the witch trusted you to be the living person to bring us all together. I am sad that I cannot be with you anymore, at least for the near future. It's weird, Courtney. A strange sensation came over me when we buried them side by side. I experienced this flashing of memories that I did not think were mine. "Am I Prudence?" I asked Dad. He smiled and shook his head. But he did say that we are bound to her by more than blood, that the living ivy connects us across these hundreds of years. In that sense, he agreed, we are one. As I write this, Dad tells me to hurry, as we must leave, but I insisted that I tell you more.

You knew, Courtney. You knew that we could not go far from the cemetery or your house. You know when we read the excerpt from Christian's journal? Remember "And the spirits that come after you will fade, will shimmer into dust, should they leave this site." There was so much that I did not understand. But Dad kept bringing me back to the ivy. "What did the witch say to Christian?" he asked. That the ivy was the symbol of Christian's love for Prudence. Christian chose the ivy first, when he carved it on Prudence's tombstone. The ivy is an unbreakable bond between them.

It was the witch, Dad told me, not Christian, who believed in the power of the spirit to live long after the body is eaten by worms. Remember what she said to

Christian? "Our spirits are made of our love, our hate, our desire—they make up our elements." When Christian spread the ashes of the ivy around his bed as the witch told him to do, it was as if the ivy and his blood were fused. Christian died—but the ivy lived on.

Dad believed that Christian did not want to tell the witch that he had moved Prudence from the old cemetery by the gravestone he had carved. It was only because of you that we learned the truth. In the meantime, the ivy grew stronger, and it learned to work with the elements to fulfill its quest. It made us from the life forces it knew. We became its children, and it taught us the covenant the witch made, to reunite them, so we all can be reunited.

But Courtney, I am happy, too, because Dad promises that I will see you again. And that you will recognize me. For now, the cats will be our bond. Care for them for me. Our mission is done.

Forever Your Friend,
Margaret

"It's not fair," I sobbed. "I didn't get to say good-bye!" I yelled at the house, angry tears blurring the words in the letter. I stood by the table with the letter in my hand and began to bawl; all of the feelings—good, bad, and scary—that had built up inside me since I had met the Geyers only a few weeks ago welled to the surface. Finally I stopped, embarrassed, even though I knew no one was around. I sniffled and wiped my eyes and squinted into the filtered sunlight that threaded through the trees. *Think,* I told myself.

Margaret was telling me that the witch had empowered the ivy to protect the spirits of Christian and Prudence and to do whatever it needed to do to bring them together. Perhaps over time it grew so strong and determined that it somehow created, with the help of the witch, Margaret and Mr. Geyer. It tried to guide them to their whereabouts, and when they failed, the ivy—and the witch—decided to use me.

I remembered Margaret's frustration at not being able to see the witch. If she and Mr. Geyer were a part of her, as they were a part of the ivy, then of course they would not be able to see her, as it would be like seeing oneself. When we were in town, it was Margaret and Mr. Geyer that people could not see because when they traveled a distance from the cemetery or the woods—from the ivy itself—they lost some of their power. The ivy was telling them, and me, that the trail to Christian and Prudence had grown cold. For whatever reason, I was the living connection that could see them all.

I looked at Christian's journal. My hand trembled as I reached for it. I expected it to crumble as I turned it over so that I could open it to the last page. I would read it all, but right now, I was looking for an answer. I opened the cover and the air smelled like attic dust. My eyes stung as I read the last entry.

"I no longer wish to live," I told her.
She nodded and touched my cheek.
Her fingers were so cold.
"When you are ready, I will burn this place," she said.
She looked at the ivy I had carved into
the walls, the floors, the furniture.
In my delirium, I had taken her at her word.
"We should leave no evidence of your spirits,"
she said, grabbing my hand.
"But first you must move Prudence to the woods.
I must bury you side by side.
You will be together forever."
I nodded.
I had no strength for discourse.

I did not tell her that Prudence was fine.
I would not allow her to be buried
in the woods like a wild animal.

I would touch fire to this place.
I would not leave my final fate
in the hands of a witch.
I would die like my Prudence.

My heart was pounding. The poor witch. She really loved Prudence and Christian and spent these last centuries striving to bring them together. Somehow she was able to bury Christian after the fire, as Margaret said in her letter. The witch was the one who led me to his grave. I thought about burning buildings I've seen on television news—how they collapse into themselves—trapping everything that is still inside. The witch could not get to Prudence, and so for all these years, the witch had struggled to bring them together. Margaret had known all along, known in her heart, that the witch was good. I felt honored that the witch had trusted me to help Christian and Prudence. *But what did I do to earn her trust?*

My heart stopped when I heard the whinny of a horse coming from the direction of the trail that led deeper into the woods. The trail that I had seen the witch stroll down the last time that I had spied her at the Geyers' house.

I froze in the door's threshold as she suddenly came into view. She was sitting sidesaddle on top of that huge black horse, her black skirt looking like its cloak. She road the magnificent creature slowly toward the house. The trees walled the path on both sides, their canopies thickly intertwined. She looked as if she were emerging from a forest portal.

She stopped where the path bled into the clearing, allowing her horse to tear hungrily at the green weeds within his reach. We stared at each other as I studied her face. Her dazzling green eyes stared right back at me. I whispered to myself as if I were reading a checklist—Margaret's black hair, green eyes, delicate nose, and stubborn chin.

"Where's Margaret?" I whispered. I wanted the witch to bring her back to me.

But the witch slowly shook her head and then placed her hand over her heart.

She nodded to me before she turned her horse around, to direct him back into the woods. She bent to whisper something in his ear, which made him shoot down the path as if a gun had fired. They soon disappeared, but I listened to his hooves hitting the path until the sound was swallowed by the woods.

Wait, I wanted to yell, but no sound would come. "Please wait," I finally did call and felt a breeze, like my mother's hand on my face. My heart was thumping again in those quick little beats, sharp and fast like the chiseling ivy. The witch wanted me to do something, but I was unsure what.

I closed the Geyers' front door and walked to the path that would take me home. When I calmed down, it would come to me, I told myself. It is just like taking a test. You always know the answers when the pressure was no longer on. That is when the orange cat—Margaret's favorite—stepped from the scrubby plants along the path to block my way, its bright, hungry eyes demanding action. I crouched down to stroke it behind its ears and it purred approvingly. I felt the tension in my chest fade away. Perhaps Margaret would always be with me.

And then I remembered the ivy was still in the cemetery and that its presence meant there was still work to be done. Christian's and Prudence's spirits—and all of the spirits who are buried there—needed protection. The witch had chosen me. She somehow knew that I could be brave and strong long before I knew it. She trusted me to help Margaret and Mr. Geyer to bring Prudence and Christian together. Despite my disappointment and the hurt that I felt in losing Margaret, I needed to keep her memory alive until we did meet again. Right then, I had to talk to my mom about what we needed to do next to save the cemetery, and to add cat food, lots of it, to our shopping list.

Aldus Manutius, a highly influential Renaissance printer, designed *Bembo* over five hundred years ago in Venice, Italy. He first used the light, easy-to-read type in the late fifteenth century publishing an essay by Pietro Bembo, an Italian scholar. The typeface soon became extremely popular throughout the country. When *Bembo* reached France, famed Parisian publisher and type designer Claude Garamond tried to duplicate it. This caused *Bembo*'s influence to spread throughout the rest of Europe. In 1929, the English Monotype company revived the *Bembo* design using books and materials set with Manutius' original fonts. By the 1980s, Monotype had created a digital version of *Bembo*, along with semi-bold and extra-bold weights and italics. This latest incarnation has solidified *Bembo* as one of the most prevalent typefaces today.

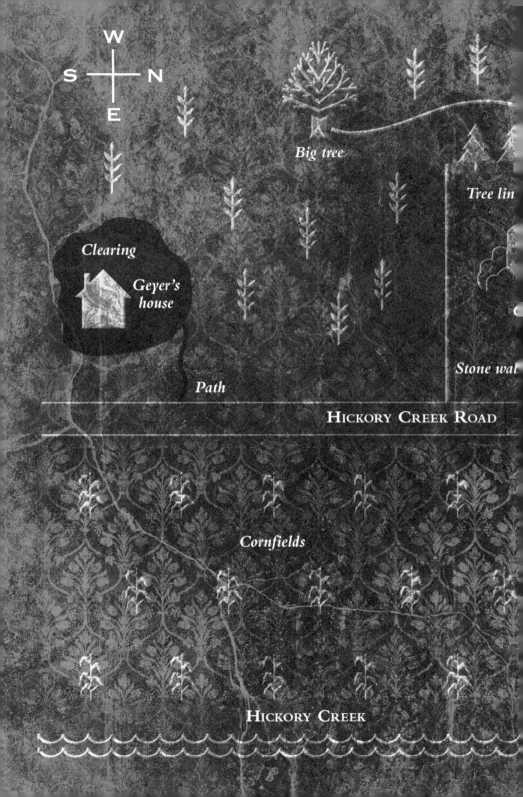